Witches Treasure

Part three:

All Hell Break Loose!

Payton Morgan

I dedicate this book to everyone who inspired me to keep going.
This one is for you.

P.M.

Contents

Chapter 1

The Cave

Alex's mind was racing at that point. In that moment he had chills running through him like a sickness. The thought of the vision he had seen was now seemingly coming true. The vision of the homecoming dance being crowded with the undead. Chasing after Alex and Liv's classmates ready to feast upon their flesh. Of all the visions that Alex was shown that one frightened him the most. More than the visions of the pastor being stabbed by a large sword by a hidden figure. Who Alex could only assume is Eleanor Shrowl herself. Worst of all, he had as far as he knew the device that could bring this vision to life. Eleanor's spell book is in his backpack. The very spell book that was responsible for the dozens of deaths. Alex used the same spell book to unintentionally murder Mike Angel, his parent's boss in the film Witches Treasure. Which still weighed heavy on his heart. While it was unintentional it was still something that lingered in his mind even now. However, that thought weighed nowhere near as much as the thought of the vision that he was shown just that morning. Alex's body started to shake with anxiety and fear. In that moment Alex did everything he could to lessen his shaking body. Liv was now looking at him as a mother would look at their child when they are frightened.

"Alex? What's wrong you're shaking" she asked. Alex could not tell her; she'd never believe him even if he did tell her everything. The sudden thought of how he told Terry when he was hurt suddenly rang in his mind. He was practically shaking in his shoes, more so than Alex was at this very moment. If Alex told Liv about the book and everything, he had experienced with it. She'd run for the hills, and Alex adored her too much to let her go like that.

"I'm fine... I just uhm" Alex's mind fluttered trying to think of a good lie to tell Liv. *I could tell her that I forgot. Though that would make me look bad.* Alex finally came up with a good lie to tell. "I just forgot to go shopping,"

"What?"

"Well, I mean I want to look for you that's all" He lied. Liv blushed when he spoke. Which in turn made Alex blush slightly.

"Oh, Alex you don't have to dress to impress me, among everyone I know here you're the only one who's ever made me..." Liv hesitated.

"Made you what?" Alex asked. There was a small silence Liv looked as though she was afraid to tell Alex anything more.

"You're the first person who has made me feel not alone, the first person who sees me as more than a pretty face. You see me as... well me" Liv explained. Alex was moved by her words. Alex had not known what kind of impact he had on her. Up until this point Alex had not thought of Liv as often as he wanted. He had been so busy with the book and everything that happened between Mike and Flora being in and out of the hospital. The last thing on his mind was his love life. A small sense of guilt rattled through his chest at this realization. Not only that but a sense of determination rang through him as well. A loving determination, a determination to keep her safe, no matter the cost.

"Tell you what, if it means that much to you after we see the cave you and I can go shopping, a new dress sounds pretty good to me don't you think?" she said jokingly. Alex chuckled and smiled.

"Okay deal," Alex said. With that said Liv kissed Alex on the cheek and continued down the road. However, now Alex realized that the further they go down this path the more and more that vision of homecoming being infested with zombies seems almost inevitable. But not only that but he also had to be sure that nothing happened to Liv. Where they were going was dangerous, regardless of what Liv said. And the worst part was Alex was packing that danger with them. But in his heart, he knows that if he is to stay with Liv, he must find the lost treasure of the Shrowl Witch.

***

After about twenty minutes of riding around, Liv finally told Alex to stop. They were now just a few miles out from the high school. Liv had Alex parked his bike behind a large oak tree that had a red ribbon wrapped around it. He and Liv both went into the forest trail which was barely visible through how much underbrush there was. Part of Alex felt as though he was Indiana Jones going through the jungle hunting for treasure. The woods were so thick they might as well have been a jungle. And like how one feels in a jungle Alex felt as though he was being watched. Like how a hunter feels watched by his prey. At this moment Alex felt like prey, but not to hungry bears or coyotes you would find in these woods. No, he fell prey to whatever lies in the cave ahead. Most people, when they go to visit caves often worry about silly things like bats or getting lost in the cave but for Alex, he was worried about something sinister, something dark, and somewhat forbidden. *I should have thought about this more clearly at home. Maybe do some research on this place before I charge in with the book.* But Alex knew that if he was to stay in Shrowl and stay with Liv he had to believe that the treasure was real. After all, after what he had seen so far with what the book had done along with the dreams and visions, he had received it be wise to assume that the treasure was real as well. *But would it be wise to use the book to find the treasure, I mean after all remember what happened to Mike.* The memory of Mike Angel's attack rang through Alex's mind like a loud bell. If it had not been as cold as it was outside Alex would still be feeling the full amount of pain, he received at the hands of Mike. What he could feel was the soreness of the whelps that had grown on his face. Alex felt as though his face was inflated like a balloon. Though if Liv was able to kiss him on the cheek, he guessed it was not as bad as he thought. Alex hears a large crack from behind him. He whipped around and saw that nothing was there. Anxiety filled him again as he felt like someone was following him. Part of him would not be surprised if someone or something was following him. The thought of that was terrifying. The wind gusted up behind him, it blew so hard that his hood blew up against his neck. He looked back in the direction the wind blew and saw that Liv was still trekking forward to the cave. Alex pauses for a second to see Liv walking so carefully yet also somehow so elegantly. She has clearly been here more than once. Alex looked back behind him and assured himself that there was nothing back there. Yet part of him knew that was a lie. Though he had to tell himself something to make himself feel better for what was ahead. Alex still had no idea what he was in store for.

***

Alex quickly caught up with Liv and followed closely behind her. If there was something following them *which there, isn't* he kept telling himself. He wasn't about to let Liv get hurt out here. They walked for almost thirty minutes. Alex had to check his watch, it was now almost eleven, which was weird considering he remembered leaving the house at around nine. *Have we only been out this long?* After that realization, Alex and Liv had finally come to a clearing. Liv stopped to tie her shoe.

As soon as she did Alex looked out into the clearing and could not believe what he was seeing. It was the canyon he had seen on the first day of school. The same canyon that he painted at home. Granted it was not as vibrant as it was at this time of day, but it was still a wonderful view, nonetheless. Alex was still able to make out the image in his head of how the sun was casting a beautiful shadow across the valley. The foliage looked more colorful than the last time he saw the canyon. There were much redder and orange trees present than there were yellow and greens. The only other thing that was as beautiful as this view was Liv's loving smile when she saw how awestruck he was at that moment.

"I know right?" Liv asked. Alex had no words, the view encapsulated him. "You know I used to come here with my dad before he died." That comment caught Alex by surprise, the moment of blissful gazing was done.

"What?" Alex asked, surprised. He looked at Liv who was now sitting on an old log. She was now gazing out into the canyon. Alex sat down next to her she did not break her gaze.

"It was four years ago," she said still looking out into the canyon. "Cancer, he had chosen not to go through chemo, he always felt that if God was ready for him then he would be ready for God." That statement broke Alex's heart, he had no idea that Liv had lost her father. Of all the ways that he could imagine a loved one dying, cancer had to be the saddest way for one to leave this world. In that moment Alex had thought about the months and or years Liv probably had to have gone through seeing her father constantly in pain, getting sicker and sicker with every passing day. He could not imagine what that would have been like if Alex had to see his family suffer that way. Alex had not lost anyone in his family, and he could not fathom what Liv must have felt when she lost her father.

"He would always take me here and tell me that he always imagined that heaven would look something like this he always called this place the gates of heaven."

"Your dad sounds like a wise man."

"He was, when he died my mother, and I cremated him and scattered him right here. So that he would be at his gates to heaven." She said just before she started to sob. Alex quickly embraced her in his arms as she sobbed into his shoulder. This lasted just a few minutes. When she was done sobbing Alex let her go and took off his jacket and wrapped it around her.

"Thank you"

"Of course, Liv," Both of them cuddled together on the log looking out into the canyon. "Liv thank you,"

"For what?" she asked.

"For taking me here, this is exactly what needed today, and from what I can see now it looks like you needed to come here as well." He chuckled.

"I should be the one thanking you Alex this is wonderful." She blushed. They locked eyes, smiled, and exchanged a long kiss. Her lips were soft against his and Alex felt like he was coarse. But she did not seem to mind. When the kiss was done, she blushed once more. Alex could not help but blush as well. His heart as well as the rest of his body began to fill up with warmth. In that moment Alex had felt like a hot air balloon being filled up with hot air. As much as Alex wanted to sit in this spot for as long as possible, he knew that they needed to get to the cave. If he ever wanted to come back to this spot and have this experience again with Liv. He needed to find the treasure of Eleanor Shrowl.

"We should get going," Alex said.

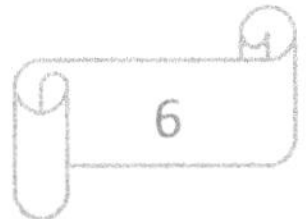

"Right," Liv said wiping her face. She stood up slowly with the jacket still wrapped around her. She offered it back to Alex, but he graciously refused. She held him by his hand as she directed them both back onto the trail to the cave. In this moment he had never felt closer to Liv than he did before. However, at that moment he also knew now exactly what he was fighting for. A chance to be with the one woman he can relate to, a chance for him to be happy and content with his life as he was back in Florida. Looking back on it, he had never found anyone of interest there. Sure, he had his friends, and he would not trade them for anything. But there was something about Liv that was so pure, so genuine, so elegantly beautiful. In that moment as her warm hand gripped his Alex's heart began to blossom and bloom. *I think I'm in love...* he said to himself in his mind. This feeling overwhelmed him the entire time they walked through the woods. Within ten minutes both had finally reached the cave of Eleanor Shrowl.

***

It had just occurred to Alex at this point that he had never exactly been inside of a cave before. He did not know exactly what to expect, he had been told about this cave a couple of times, yet he had yet to see this cave in the flesh, let alone a picture of it. The cave stood on the side of a large cliff base. From where Alex and Liv were standing the cave looked as though it was a large gaping mouth on the side of the mountain. It had large rock formations across the bottom and the tops of the opening. *God, it almost looks like teeth!* As they moved closer to the cave the more uneasy Alex felt his original feeling of warmth and comfort that Liv had given him just a couple of minutes ago was now replaced with the sudden urge to run. But he knew he couldn't, if he was to stay in Shrowl and stay with Liv he needed to go in there.

"What do you think?" Liv asked. Just like how he saw the canyon earlier Alex was lost for words. This was seen by Liv who giggled at the shocked look on his face. "Come on," she said while grabbing his hand again. They were now at the entrance of the cave which up close Alex could see that it stretched for miles. As they made their way inside just as was described to Alex the ceiling of the cave glittered and shined as if the night sky was shining down upon them. The legend goes that that is where the treasure is. It is said that the reason they shine so bright is because before Eleanor Shrowl died, she had used a spell to hide the treasure inside the very walls of the cave. As Alex looked around, the cave walls were almost completely covered in graffiti and trash. Part of him was on edge about being in here, not because this was his first time being in a cave or the overwhelming feeling that he was followed by something or someone. But this place seemed like the kind of place where homeless people would come to crash. He was surprised he did not see any large barrels with burnt soot at the bottom of it. Then again Alex's interpretation of homelessness was based on what he had seen in movies.

"What do you think?" Liv asked. Alex could hear her voice echo around him.

"Wow..." he spoke softly. With that said Alex was still able to hear his echo come back to him throughout the cave. He looked at Liv who seemed amused. He then clasped his hands around his mouth and shouted into the cave. "WOW!!!" Just like before his voice came racing back to him as well as the rest of the cave. Liv laughed when she saw him do this.

"You look like a kid when he sees candy."

"Sorry, it's just I've never experienced anything like this before."

"What do you mean?"

"Not a lot of things like in Florida other than the beach,"

"Well, you're lucky I have yet to see the ocean," Liv added. Alex looked at her surprised.

"What?"

"Well, my mom works two jobs and there's not a lot of time for her and I to travel, though I would like to go. But for now, I have this to settle for" Liv answered. As wonderful as this cave looked to Alex in his mind, everyone must see the ocean at least once in their life. He remembered the first time he was at the beach. It was when he was four years old, it was in the afternoon his parents had just got off work when they decided to take him before it got dark. The water was too cold for him to swim, but he remembered seeing the sky and the horizon of the ocean. Its vastness, its glory. The sky was almost golden with hues of red and yellow, the clouds added a sense of texture to this glorious view. He remembered how it made him feel at that moment. How when looking out into that view he knew that the world was much bigger than he ever thought possible. In that moment he saw the beauty of the world, beauty that he wanted to capture and keep with him wherever he went. Looking back at that memory he believed that was the moment that he decided what he wanted to be. Someone who could capture that glorious image and share it to those who unfortunately are unable to see something as glorious as that moment. In a way he felt as though it was his duty to spread the beauty of the world to everyone. But in this moment the only person he wanted to share the glorious image of the endless escape of the ocean was Liv.

"Looks like I am just gonna have to take you to the beach at some point" Alex said jokingly. Liv did not seem so confident when he said that. Matter of fact part she looked as though she was going to cry again. "Hey, what's wrong?" Alex asked. She looked at him, her eyes were glassy, she was on the brink of tears.

"Sorry, it's just the last person who told me that was my dad, just before he..." she said before sobbing into Alex's arms. Alex held her as tight as he could, he felt as though he could ore to help her in that moment. But nothing was coming to mind, all that he could do was hold her in his arms.

"Liv, I'm so sorry I—"

"It's okay, you didn't know" she answered. There was a brief silence between the two of them. Tears streaked down her face as she looked into his eyes. Alex gently wiped away her tears and spoke softly.

"I'd like to know more if you'd let me?" Liv smiled and kissed Alex softly.

"I'd like that very much" Liv answered. They kissed once more. Behind him Alex heard the clomping of shoes, before he could even turn around to see who it was, he felt something strike his head. Pain had rung through his head like a bell, his blow happened so fast and so hard that Alex's ears started to ring once again. The only thing that Alex could hear through the ringing was the muffled cries of Liv screaming.

***

Once again Alex found himself in the forest in his dreams again. The trees seemed to be taller than they were before. Alex looked up and could not see the tops of them. Yet somehow, he knew that these trees were unlike the trees he had seen in his previous dream. The bark of these trees was black. Alex felt the closest one and he felt it burn his skin. As if it was internally smoldering. Alex looked ahead and saw that the trail that was once there was much more open. He looked around and saw dead animals through the bushes of the forest. Gray rabbits, squirrels, and large deer slumped over with their bodies opened as if they were feasted upon by a ravenous beast. Alex did not want to see this sight anymore, so he quickly made his way through the trail. However, he was still unable to escape the horrors he had left behind the trail only offered more destruction and death as he ran through hoping, and praying that this would end. As he ran through the forest of his mind, he couldn't help but look back at the events that preceded his arrival in this dreamscape. He remembered sharing a tender kiss with Liv and a second later he was here again. But why? Why would he be back here? The last time he was here was when he fell asleep in the car just before he had his altercation with Mike.

"What the hell happened to this place?" he asked himself as he continued through the dead woods of his mind. The more he walked the more he saw nothing but death. It was only yesterday when he dreamt of this place, he remembered how lush and beautiful it was, how the animals frolicked peacefully. Alex had always considered this place his home away from home, but now it looks as though someone had gone out of their way to destroy the one place he feels at peace. One thing Alex could not shake at this moment was the same feeling he felt when walking through the woods with Liv. He still had this overwhelming feeling that he was being followed by something. *But there's nothing here,* he thought. Alex stopped and slowly turned around. The trail that he was going through was gone. Though he did see a hill that he knew for a fact he did not pass over. This place was always a flattened stretch of land, there were no hills, or divots in the ground. Yet somehow there was a large hill that stood almost ten yards away from where he was standing. The wind suddenly began to howl as if there was an approaching storm coming. He looked around him and the dead branches of the trees began to shiver and shake with the wind. He looked back at the hill and saw something he thought he would never see again. His eyes bulged and his skin began to shrivel as he stood there in fear of the black shroud of smoke that came from the book. The same shroud he had seen just that morning. Alex was frozen in fear he didn't know whether to run or not. Part of him knew that running would be futile, this was his dream. *Wait, this is my dream, this thing can't hurt me, right?*

"I WAAAANNT THE BOOOKK!!!" the shroud of smoke exclaimed loudly as it drew closer to him. It was at this point that Alex began to run for his life. Alex's mind was now racing with fear and panic as he traversed the forest as best as he could. He could now hear crunching leaves and branches behind him. He knew that whatever this thing was it was coming for him, and it was not going to stop until it got him. As he ran, he thought of one thing, *the beach!* He remembered the last time he saw this thing in his dream Eleanor was there, maybe she was there still. With that thought in mind, he ran faster than he had ever run before. Within minutes he was finally able to make it to the beach where a person was along the shore. Alex caught a glimpse of the once beautiful sky he saw before was now crimson and black. As if the sky was bleeding, dying, and turning into something dark, something putrid. Alex could see this person sitting on the shore. He quickly rushed over to them.

"Miss Shrowl help me please something is—AHH!!!"

The person sitting was not Eleanor at all, it was Terry who had tears rolling down his face. He was still wearing the clothes he had on yesterday at school however these clothes looked torn and ragged. Terry looked at Alex, his face was red and beaten as if he had gone another round with Tank.

"Alex, you have to kill me," he said grimly.

"What? Terry, what are you talking about?"

"She's got me... you must stop her before she kills you too. You must kill me."

"Who's got you, Terry?" Before he could answer across Terry's right shoulder was a bony black hand. Alex took a step back as Terry whimpered in fear. Behind Terry stood the black smoke creature that pursued Alex through the forest. The creature let out a menacing roar and sent Alex screaming. Through the screams, he heard Terry's voice once again.

"HELP ME!!!!!" Alex screamed once more as the shroud of smoke dragged Terry out into the bloody ocean of his mind and before Alex could go after him, he had awoken screaming for his friend. His friend who he now believes is in grave danger.

***

Alex was now back in the cave. Only now it was not as bright out as it was before. He looked at his watch which to his surprise read 4:30. *It was almost 11 when we came here!* Fear and panic quickly rushed through him with this realization. As he tried to get up, he heard the crackling of fire along with the sound of rain pouring. It echoed and moaned throughout the cave, just like every other sound that passes through here. Alex tried to sit up, but he felt his head feel heavy as if it was made from bricks. As he tried to move, he began to see stars along with that he felt a massive amount of pain rush through his skull. As he tried to move, he heard footsteps approach him, Alex's vision was fading in and out but by the sound of these steps whoever was walking towards him was huge. In a split-second, Alex felt a new wave of pain in his skull this time through his hair. Whoever this person was, they were now dragging Alex by his hair to what he assumes is a bonfire. Alex screamed as he kicked and squirmed to try and loosen the grip of whoever had a hold of him, but it only brought on more pain. When the person finally let go Alex heard a familiar voice, a voice that sent a chill right down his spine.

"What's up fuckboy!!!" said Tank grimly.

"Tank, what are you—where's Liv?" Alex asked. He looked up at Tank who was now walking around the bonfire menacingly. He chuckled slightly and pointed across the fire in front of Alex. It was at this point Alex's vision came back fully. He could now see that Liv was beaten and bruised, her once beautiful hair and makeup were now disheveled and ruined. She had streaks of mascara tears across her eyes and rolled down to her chin. She was tied up and gagged with a bandana. Fury and rage-filled Alex's inside like a fire. He felt as though he was a bomb with a fuse lit. As he watched in horror what he had seen Tank continued to laugh maniacally.

"YOU SICK SON OF A BITCH!!!" Alex shouted as he charged at Tank which was promptly met by a choke slam from Tank. Alex's ears began to ring again. He could hear the muffled shouting Tank was saying. He could not make out concise words, but he knew he was saying something. Alex looked again at Liv who was afraid in her eyes. Tank grabbed Alex by the throat and picked him up. Once again, he could see stars, his legs were weak, and he could barely stand without a moment to catch his breath Alex felt a large blow to his gut as well as a couple in his face. The face that had already gone through not one, not two, but three beatings within the same week. And was about to go through its fourth.

"YOU GOT ME EXPELLED YOU LITTLE SHITSTAIN!!!" Tank shouted as he continued whaling down on Alex. "AND NOW YOU TRY TO STEAL MY GIRL!!! MY GIRL!!!" Tank was throwing jabs from almost every direction. "Your gonna fuckin' die and I am gonna make sure she watches and sees for herself that nobody messes with THE TANK!!!" Tank continued with his beating and in that moment, Alex knew that nothing was stopping him from carrying out Tank's mission. The beating did not last as long as the last couple though Alex did feel new bones being shattered in this encounter. The only thing that he could make out in this beating was the muffled cries of Liv as she had to sit there and watch as Tank annihilated Alex. When the beating was done Alex felt as though he was a pile of broken parts. Like a marionette puppet with its lines cut. Part of him was thankful that it was just Tank if he had brought the other guys that beat the shit out of him when he first came to Shrowl chances are he probably would not be alive right now. However, he did not think that was going to last very long.

"Now let's see what the love birds were planning on doing shall we?" Tank said as he ripped off Alex's backpack. *OH, SHIT THE BOOK!!!* Alex thought, he tried to move his arm to reach the book, this was seen by Tank who stomped down on Alex's arm. Alex screamed once more as he clutched his newly broken arm. Tank emptied the contents of the bag onto the floor of the cave. Most of it was folders, binders, and a couple of journals with some doodles Alex did in class. But the one thing, the only Alex did not want Tank to find fell promptly onto the floor of the cave. The brown leather-bound book of spells. The same book that Eleanor Shrowl had used almost three hundred years ago. The same book that brought the end to Mike Angel just the night before. The same book that Alex thought would be his salvation in finding the treasure and staying with Liv.

"The hell is this?" Tank asked. Tank picked up the book and flipped through the pages. Alex tried again to get the book but before he could Tank began to read from the book aloud. "Mendiclus Gretis?" Tank was still in a sling from his "basketball accident" he and Terry caused just a couple of days ago but when he read that spell. There was a loud snap that came from Tank's arm.

"OW!!! WHAT THE HELL WAS—hey, my arm!!!" Tank was now able to fully use his right arm again. Alex looked at Liv whose eyes were wider than an owl's.

"No..." Alex muttered. Tank looked at him and looked back at the book then back at Alex.

"It was you..." Tank said. Alex slowly tried to crawl away from Tank as he approached. "You were the reason I broke my arm; you were the one that made us lose the game. You were the reason I was made a fool in front of everyone!!!"

"Ta-nk plea-se" Alex pleaded. Alex then looked at Liv who was now starting to realize the same thing as Tank was.

"I don't know what this book is, but let's see how you like it!!!"

"No..." Alex said.

"Let's see how about Kamarro!" Without hesitation, a large rock bashed against Alex's head. "You know it just occurred to me I can hurt you as much as I want, Mendiclus Gretis" Just like the last time Alex had this spell done on him instantly his body healed. Though in his case the healing process hurt just as much as the beating that came before. Alex screamed in both pain and delight as his body slowly but surely healed itself. As soon as it was done Tank spoke once again. "Weivelo beru!!!" This was a different spell that Alex had not used before. He didn't know what to expect. Before he could make a move for the book Alex was now levitating in midair. As he floated Tank began to laugh hysterically. "Look babe I'm David fuckin' Copperfield!!!"

"Tank that book is dangerous you need to put it down now!!!"

"And waste such power? Not a chance Kamarro!!!" Just like before more rocks slammed against Alex's face which left him spinning in the air. His ears began to ring once more, but through the ringing, he could hear the muffled cries of Tank laughing his ass off. This beating was much worse than the one he had just gone through. This one seemed to last hours and the worst part was that every time Tank hurt Alex, he would heal him again just so he could do it again. It was torture, in this beating Alex had been thrown around the walls of the cave, had numerous rocks hurled across his face, and slammed into the floor as if he had gone skydiving without a parachute. Each time he felt as though he was going to die but then Tank would bring him back from the brink of death just so he could hurt him worse than he did the last. Not only that but to add insult to injury he had to listen to Tank's squealing laugh every time he would use the book on Alex. Along with that Liv could only sit there and watch as Alex was being tossed around like a ragdoll.

After what seemed like hours of torture Tank had finally had his fill and decided to cut the party short.

"Okay, no more games, Mendiclus Gretis" he had healed Alex once again though he was still floating above him was a large sharp stalactite that hung from the roof of the cave. Alex was still floating upwards at that moment he knew that Tank was planning to skewer him like a kabob on the large rocky spike and be done with him.

"TANK PLEASE DON'T DO THIS!!!" he shouted as he shouted, he saw Liv screaming through her gag pleading for him not to do it as well.

"NOBODY MESSES WITH THE TANK!!!!" Alex screamed as he slowly approached the spike waiting for it to plunge into his body, he closed his eyes and waited for death to come quickly.

"Enough," said a disembodied voice. With that said Alex peered open his eyes and saw that he was millimeters away from the hanging stalactite he looked and saw that someone was standing at the entrance of the cave. As this person approached the fire it became clearer who this person was.

"Terry fairy?" Tank said confused.

"Terry?" Alex said confused as well. Alex's view was not great, he was looking for him upside down though from what he could see Terry was still wearing the same clothes as he had on the day before. The same clothes he had on when he was in Alex's dreamscape. At that moment Alex thought back to what he said. *'She's got me... you must stop her before she kills you too.'* Something was not right, something in him told him that the person that had just walked into the cave was not his friend.

"Get lost fairy, or you'll be next!!!" Tank said defiantly.

"TANK RUN!!!" Alex shouted. Without hesitation, Tank was slammed against the wall by an unseen force with that blow he dropped the book dangerously close to the fire. Along with that Alex was sent falling to his death in the cave. Alex's screams were cut short when he felt something catch him and lower him back down safely. He looked at Tank who was now still pinned to the wall. Alex quickly ran towards the fire, grabbed the book then ran to Liv and untied her.

"Oh Alex," she said as she embraced him tightly.

"It's okay Liv, I'll explain everything I promise" Alex reassured her. He looked back at Terry who was now by the fire staring at him blankly.

"Thank you, Ter, —" Liv said before she was cut off by Alex.

"Who the hell are you?" Alex said sharply. Terry half smiled as he smiled his eyes went cold, and slowly began to turn black.

"Wouldn't you like to know pal?" Terry said defiantly.

"I ask again WHO THE HELL ARE YOU!!!" Alex shouted.

"Alex, what are you doing?" Liv asked.

"That's not Terry" Alex responded. Liv looked at Terry as if he was a stranger.

"Give me the book Alex" Terry spoke grimly. His voice sounded much deeper than it usually was at that moment. Both Alex and Liv knew this when they both looked at each other. Alex shook his head now and held the book tighter. Terry spoke once more. "GIIIVE MEEEE THEEE BOOOOOK!!!!" he shouted. As he spoke Terry's body began to change, his skin began to turn crimson and black, and he looked as though it was now made from burnt wood. Alex could see the fire coursing through Terry's cheeks as his black eyes darted at him. As they started Terry began to speak once more, only it was not words he was saying at all. No this had to be a spell of some kind. It was one Alex had never heard of before.

"Verticus Klatros Deliflushstro!!!!" the creature that was once Terry shouted. As it finished Alex and Liv felt the ground beneath them start to shake and rumble. Behind them, they heard a thump and saw that whatever was holding Tank against the wall was gone.

"Alex, what the hell is going on?" Tank asked. Before Alex could even answer him several yards away in the darkness of the cave Alex, Liv, and Tank all saw bright red lights that looked as though they were red lightning bugs buzzing their way. As they grew closer towards the fire the three stood there in horror by what looked like a small army of the undead. Their flesh practically dripped off their bones. Some of them looked to be wearing pilgrim or Amish clothing. They stood there staring at them. Alex looked at Terry who was now smiling menacingly.

"Get them my children..." Terry spoke bluntly. Alex looked back at the horde of zombies behind them and with that said they began to charge at full speed.

"RUUUNNN!!!!"

Chapter 2

Terry

It was almost three in the morning when Terry came home from work the night before. He came in wearing the same clothes he had worn to school that day. Only now they were drenched in sweat. Terry worked at a steel mill a couple of towns over. They offered late night shifts and Terry felt as though he needed to put himself out there if he was going to get out of Shrowl. He had aspired to leave Shrowl for some time. It started when his mother had died almost six years ago, two years before he came out of the closet. She had died in a car accident; he did not know the details of the crash because his father at the time refused to tell him about it. It was a safe assumption that it was not a pretty crash, considering her funeral was a closed casket. Before Terry's mother passed his father Gus was the kindest man God had ever seen. He would volunteer at food banks, give out turkeys during Thanksgiving, and support the troops in their fundraisers. Hell, he even went so far as to do a charity marathon for breast cancer. The only person his father knew at the time who had gone through cancer was Liv's father who sadly lost his fight years ago. But tonight, Gus was now a hollow shell of a man. Who was now passed out on the couch drunk. Almost every night he would have at least two or three beers. Gus did not work a lot most of the time when he wasn't at work he would be sitting in his chair and watching TV. It didn't matter what was on, he would just stare blankly at that screen. Like a moth looking at a bright light. *A drunken moth* Terry thought. As he limped through the living room. The shift Terry had just come from was not the best. He had dropped a piece of pipe on his foot just before he left. It wasn't a large pipe, but it left a whopping bruise on his foot. In and out his foot would throb with pain, anytime he put any kind of pressure on the ball of the foot (where the pipe landed) it would send an aching pain through his foot and into his ankle. *If I had that book right now my foot wouldn't be hurting as badly as it is right now. Damn you, Alex.*

"It's too dangerous" Terry mocked as he limped across the living room. He had grabbed one of the quilts his mother had made and draped it over his father in his chair. Terry looked around the chair and saw almost ten empty beer cans scattered about. "Good lord Dad," he said to himself. Ever since his mother passed Terry's father has been in a constant depressed state. The only thing that dulled the pain of the loss of his wife was the bottom of a bottle. Which he met with regularly, more regularly than his son. Whom he might as well as disowned when he came out of the closet.

Terry expected this to happen, his mother was much more tolerant of him than his father. Who had grown up in a devout protestant household. The most interaction Terry would receive from 'dear old dad' would be one word when he eventually wakes up from his drunken slumbers, 'Hey'. After that, all he would receive afterward would be scornful side eyes and judgment-fueled looks of disappointment. A small part of Terry hated his father, but he chose not to let the hate flow through him. When he thinks of his father, he thinks of all the good he had done that outweighs the bad. When Terry looks at his father on this night, he sees not only a broken man, but he sees the man who took him out for ice cream every last day of school. He sees the man who showed him how to ride a bike and throw a ball (even though he didn't even want to) but it was still a good father-son moment that rings clear in his mind. Not only did that memory cross his mind but so did one of the last memories he had shared with both his parents. One of Terry's mother's last requests was that they see the ocean. It was the only time he had ever seen the ocean and part of Terry wanted it to remain that way. He remembered the picnic he and his father laid out for his mother. How much she loved eating all her favorite foods and seeing the world encapsulated in splendid beauty. They had come just at sundown, so the sky was a wonderful array of reds and oranges. At that moment Terry remembered what he told himself when he was on that beach. *This is what heaven will look like,* with that thought he found comfort in knowing that his mother was going to a better place. Along with that Terry remembered the sight of both his mother and father looking out into the sea as they fully embraced the beauty they were beheld. In that moment, Terry knew that his father was coming to that same conclusion, though since then he has not been handling the death of his beloved healthily.

Terry went back into his room, which was littered with plant life, books, and neon lights that draped the ceiling. One thing that Terry prided himself on was how peaceful his room was. The ceiling of his room had cotton and neon light across it. When the lights could come on it would look like glowing clouds were in his room. He had also set up a motion sensor every time he would come into his room, he had a speaker that would play some meditation music. The kind of music that did not have any words but, the kind of music that would make the mind tingle and make one feel as though they were floating. Above everything else Terry craved peace. Peace of mind, body, and soul, not only that but he craved acceptance from anyone. For a while, he thought he found that kind of acceptance through Alex, but now after their fight, he does not know. Though looking back at what he had experienced with Alex he could not have been more pleased with himself. *You made a friend, not just any friend, a friend who accepted you for you. Not only that, but he showed you that Magik is real, and it is powerful.*

"You must be powerful," he told himself confidently as he looked at himself in the full-body mirror, he had hanging off the back of the door. That thought lingered as he changed into his pajamas and got into his bed. Before he goes to sleep every night, he takes a couple of minutes to meditate. It's something that has always helped him get to sleep faster. If he did not take this time he would be up till morning. During this time, he would take his time and relax to the point where he would pass out just as he would lay his head. However, tonight did not need that much effort, he was already physically exhausted from work. Meditation was his way of cleansing his demons of the day that he had and starting fresh the next. Though often scars are left behind from those days. For this one, it was Alex and how he treated Terry to save him from Tank. You would think he would be grateful to Terry for practically saving his life but somehow, he's the bad guy for doing exactly what Tank deserved in that moment. Even though he deserved far worse. If it were up to Terry at that moment, he would have ripped Tank limb by limb if he wanted to use that book. The same book that he had used the night of the homecoming basketball game where he broke Tank's arm using Magik. Terry remembered the feeling he had when he used that spell on Terry. How relieved he was when he heard the bones snap as he watched. Sure, it was gruesome, but if everyone got to see what Tank had done to him over the years they would not have reacted as they did.

As he lay there in his bed Terry thought back to all the times Tank and beaten him to a pulp. How, in several cases, he was inches from death thanks to that insufferable redneck and his idiot friends. The worst beating, he had ever received from Tank was when he finally came out of the closet. He was lucky to still be able to walk and eat properly after the altercation he had with Tank. If he had beaten him anymore, he would have had some sort of brain damage. If there was one thing that Tank hated more than, nazis and liberals it was homosexuals. And he used Terry as a punching bag to show just how much he despised them. Terry remembered the night he got his long-awaited revenge on Tank. How good it felt to beat him to a pulp as he did so to him. And the best part was not only was he doing it with someone who understood him completely, but Tank had no earthly idea that he was the one doing it in the first place! *If I only held on to that book! I should have never let Alex have that book!* Terry thought as he lay there looking up at the glowing cloud ceiling above him. As he lay there his eyes started to grow heavy, the exhaustion began to come to him in waves, and in no time, Terry was now finally at rest.

***

As he rested Terry dreamt of that beach where he had seen his mother. Only in this case, the beach he was on was much different than the one he visited. The sand looked almost pink. However, it was mostly due to how the sky was overhead. Terry looked out at the sunset sky which had large hues of red, orange, and yellow streaked across the sky. It was as though the sky itself was a swirl of warm, comfortable colors. Terry felt a warm breeze brush through his arms and back. He took a deep breath, and, at that moment, he could not be any more at peace than he was at that moment. He looked ahead and saw someone standing on the beach with their feet in the water.

"Mom?" he said as he looked at this person. Whoever this person was had a large scarf over their head much like how his mom had when they came to visit the beach. However, this person was not wearing the same clothes his mother wore the last time he was there. This person was wearing a white shirt that was tucked into an old grey dress which as Terry examined as he got closer looked to be torn. "Mom? Is that you? Terry asked. As he approached from behind. Something inside him did not want to look at his mother at that moment. The last time he had seen his mother's face was when she was practically skin in bones on her hospital bed. Terry could not bear to stare into the face of his sickly mother. As he stood there next to this woman staring out into the vast expanse of water, he spoke to her not breaking eye contact ahead of him. "Mom, I'm sorry, I'm so so sorry about Dad, he just misses you so much. And—so do I. I've been trying to move on, but you and I both know how hard that could be for someone like me." There was a small silence, nothing was said at that moment. Terry continued gazing out into the ocean and spoke once again.

"I made a friend Mom, a good friend who helped me when those mean boys at school would beat on me. But I messed it all up, but I guess that's what I am best at nowadays." Just as Terry was done speaking the woman next to him finally spoke to him.

"Your mother loves you very much Terry," the woman said. The woman did not sound like Terry's mother at all it was at this point Terry finally looked at the face of the woman he was standing next to. He gasped as he looked into the face of a young woman around Terry's age. She had brown eyes and brown hair. Her face was placid, and her complexion looked as though she was sick or worse dying. Terry took a few steps backward as he stared at this woman.

"Wh-who are you?" Terry asked.

"My name is Eleanor, Eleanor Shrowl," Terry's eyes bulged, a shiver went down his spine and that warm breeze that he had felt before switched to a shivering sweep that engulfed Terry.

"You-you're the Shrowl Witch!!!" Terry shouted. Eleanor shushed him and nodded.

"I am no witch, but you should run Terry" Eleanor explained. Terry looked at her perplexed.

"Why?" he asked. Eleanor's eyes bulged as she looked behind Terry. When Terry saw this, he instantly turned around and saw a hooded figure approach them along the shoreline.

"You need to run! Now Terry before she takes you and destroys us all!!!" Eleanor shouted. Terry looked back at Eleanor. "RUN TERRY RUN!!!!"

***

Terry did exactly what he was told he ran back away from the shore where he found a large dense forest. As he made his way deeper into this forest, he could hear the distant calls of Eleanor shouting for him to run as the shrouded figure drew closer. His mind was fluttering with panic and terror as he traversed through the woods desperately trying to get away from the creature that was following him. As he ran his mind was racing with questions. *Who the hell is that? Why is Eleanor Shrowl in my dreams, and what did she mean she was no witch?* Those questions had to wait as he was practically running for his life in his mind. This felt too real to be a nightmare, Terry has had nightmares before, but nothing compared to anything like this before. No this had a real threat behind it, but not only that but whenever Terry had a nightmare even if it was something as small as him showing up to school dressed in nothing but the clothes, he had worn at Coachella he would always wake up. This felt more real than anything he had experienced before. Which meant his life was in grave danger and he had to find a way out of his waking nightmare. He had run for what felt like hours, his heart was skipping beats per second. He had never felt this level of terror before, the only time he came close to this feeling was the latest beating he had gotten from Tank and his goons. Though at that time he had Alex there to heal him with Magik. But he no longer had the book, and he was facing something much more powerful than him. And that very thing is hunting him down as if he were a deer being hunted by drunk rednecks.

Terry could not run any longer. If he did, he would have busted a lung. All was quiet now in the woods. However that made him even more on edge. Normally in woods such as these, you would hear something, the chirp of crickets, the buzzing of mosquitoes. Hell, even leaves falling off their branches make a distinct noise, but Terry does not hear a sound. The only thing that was heard was the ringing in his ears from the silence. That silence did not break for a solid minute. A loud crack occurred just five yards away from Terry who was resting on a tree. Terry jumped and covered his mouth so that he would not scream. The cause of that crack was a small rabbit. Which looked at Terry with a curious gaze, a sense of relief swelled over Terry when seeing that delicate creature. Terry took this time to examine where exactly he was this forest looked as though you would find it somewhere high in the mountains, not by a beach. But he guessed that there were no rules for how this dreamscape looked. If anything, Terry would have preferred to be back on the beach. But that would have made him easy prey for the thing that was still hunting him. He hid and slunk around the trees and bushes careful not to make a sound. Behind him, the rabbit trailed him. Terry began to creep further into the woods to try and find a better hiding spot.

As he walked Terry glanced behind him and saw that was not the only thing that was following him. A small deer was now following him along with the rabbit, not only that but a couple of squirrels. A little part of him felt like he was Snow White with how many woodland creatures want to be in his company. It was at this point that he started to worry. Not because he was being tailed by these animals but because not once, when he was walking through the woods did, he hear any of them behind him. It was only when he looked forward that he heard something. A small growl, his legs began to shake, and his lips began to tremble when he crept his head back around to the small animals behind him. Their blank black eyes were now crimson red, and they all began to growl as if they were hungry rottweilers waiting to chow down on a nice juicy steak.

"Oh, come on!!!" Terry said to himself as the animals dashed him. Without a moment to lose Terry was back to running for his life again. He leaped and swerved through bushes and hills as the demonic woodland creatures pursued him.

"What the fuck! What the fuck! WHAT THE FUCK!!!!" Terry shouted as he made his way through the woods. He could not believe what he was doing at that very moment. He is being chased through the woods by small seemingly harmless woodland animals who now want to rip him to pieces. In the blink of an eye, Terry was sideswiped by a large demonic stag which knocked him down on the ground. The stag roared at Terry's face. Terry let out a horrendous scream as the stag took a large bite from his right shoulder. Pain, unlike anything he had felt before coursed through his shoulder. In a panic with his free hand, Terry shuffled around the ground to try and find something, anything that could save him. He felt something hard and gripped it tightly. He did not care what it was, he used it to batter the deer off of him. Which he successfully did, it appears Terry found a large stick that broke over the savage deer's head knocking it unconscious. Terry heard scuttling leaves and twigs. The other creatures were still after him. Terry clutched his bleeding shoulder as he made his escape once again.

***

Terry had a hard time traversing through the woods. His vision was becoming blurred, and the entire right side of his chest was throbbing in pain. Tears streaked down his face as he ran. He did not care where he was running, he knew that if he heard anything even if it was something small, he had to run. As he ran, he noticed that the trees were slowly becoming less dense. He continued in this direction and before he knew it Terry was back on the beach where he first arrived. Only now the beach was much more different than how it was when he was here last. The sky was now crimson red, and the clouds were black, the sea was now a mixture of red and black, and as Terry moved closer to it he noticed that it was now boiling. Dead fish floated to the top of the water, which gave off a horrible smell that made Terry gag. As Terry stood there in horror, he saw at last the creature that had been hunting him. It was a tall black hooded person. As they walked a black mist trailed off their black robe. Terry had tried to run once again but the sand beneath his feet quickly held onto him, planting him into the ground. Terry tried desperately to free his legs from this trap, but no amount of struggling seemed to be enough to loosen the grip it had on him. Terry looked back and saw that the hooded figure was now drawing closer. His panicked mind went into overdrive as he tugged furiously at his legs.

"Come on! COME ON!!!" He said as he tugged and pulled. It did not matter if he felt a cold breeze behind him, in that moment he stopped cold. The creature was now directly behind him. Terry could not bring himself to look, he was too terrified to do so. He felt a cold bony hand grasp his wounded shoulder. Terry did not even wince in pain due to how scared he was. Urine slowly crept down his leg as he was now no longer in control of his bodily functions. He felt something brush his left shoulder and he began to shake violently. "Ple-please don't hurt me..." he sobbed.

"Oh, sweet boy, you'll do just fine." Said a chilling female voice.

"Wh--who are you?" Terry asked.

"I'll show you..." in an instant, Terry felt the other hand of this woman grasp his head and he was instantly transported to a small cottage in the middle of the woods. Inside was a middle-aged woman with a familiar-looking book and a cauldron with thick white smoke bellowing out from it. The woman had brown hair with several peaks of gray poking through. She was slender, had a square-like face, and somehow had smoother skin than anyone Terry had ever seen. He then heard the creature behind him speak once more.

"There once was a lonely girl who had stumbled onto power that reviled God himself. When she learned more of this power the young girl thought that she could become a god herself. The book she had found came to her one night when she had wanted to contact her long lost mother on her eighteenth birthday." In the smoke of the cauldron, Terry was shown glimpses of what this woman was speaking of he saw a little girl be given a book, a book that seemed all too familiar. In that moment a chill raced through him.

"Instead of speaking with her mother she was given a book bound in human flesh and inked in blood. In it were spells and incantations that brought her many things. One of the first spells this little girl used was one to dismember her drunken father. She then used this Magik to grant herself the best life could offer." Around the cottage he saw that it was very well furnished, it was as if a king had lived there. "But nothing seemed to satisfy the girl, she had gone town to town taking everything they had to offer, and the best part was they never knew where their money had gone! But all of that came to ruin when some girls in a small village called Salem caught her enchanting a farmer into robbing their pastor." Terry was being shown all of this through the smoke of the cauldron. It was like a projected movie through a smoke screen. "To conceal her deeds, she offered her power to the girls who in turn used it to slaughter anyone that was deemed abnormal. However, there was one girl named Priscilla who had blabbed of the magical little girl who had been robbing the small town of Salem blind while they were so busy trying to decide who would face a noose next for witchcraft. When the girl was discovered, she ran and using her magik built herself a haven and enchanted it so that nobody would ever find it." Terry looked around and saw that this was no ordinary cottage, it was a safe house for dark Magik. "As the girl laid low, she studied the book for decades honing her practice for something that would finally bring her the power she so desperately craved." Terry gulped as he was afraid of what was going to be said next.

"The girl had found a spell that would unleash a swarm of subservient monsters, but this spell required something, something in her long life she had yet to find. Silver, in its purest form, silver is one of the only metals on Earth that could be enchanted the way she needed it to be. But there was none to find. Until she had gone out one day and found a small girl in a blacksmith's shop gazing at a pure silver sword!" At that moment Terry knew exactly who he was talking about.

"Eleanor Shrowl..."

"Yes, poor Eleanor, I knew that she was my only way to retrieve that blade. Not only that but I figured if I were to have that blade, I might as well have the rest of the village's gold as well!" Terry was then shown Eleanor being killed next to a lake by a woman who barely had any clothes on her. He gasped as Eleanor's body finally sank to the bottom of the pond. After that, the woman responsible threw the knife into the pond and ran off. After the girl was gone the brown-haired woman revealed herself from behind a tree. She then reached into a small satchel tossed a handful of salt into the pond and muttered an incantation. After she had the water then began to glow blue. Terry's eyes began to bulge out of his head by what he was seeing.

"Raising the dead is easy, anyone could do that, but if I were to use this girl, I would need her to have full control of herself and that took time. So, I waited by that salt-filled pond for months until finally, the girl emerged" Just as she spoke Terry was shown Eleanor being brought back to life.

"Oh my god..." he said.

"I could not reveal myself just yet, but I could reveal my book and let the girl do all the work for me. So, before she reached the shore I placed my book there for her to find and well..."

"You used her..."

"Oh no, my dear boy she was just a poor animal caught in my trap," In that instant, a distinct memory came to mind. One of the first memories Terry had was when Alex had shown him the book. On the first page, it said that it belonged to someone.

"You're the original owner of the book, aren't you?" Terry asked.

"I am, and my dear boy so will you because you and I will finally fulfill my destiny!!!" She cried.

"Which is?" Just then Terry was shown another vision of what was to come. The smoke from the cauldron surrounded him and he was shown visions of creatures he had never seen before horned creatures with black skin and large horns. Creatures that seemed to be part man and part beast. Each of them was more bloodthirsty than the next.

"To unleash my army of demons, and monsters and claim this world as my own! And you Terry will see to it that becomes a reality."

"No..." Terry said through his tears.

"Sorry, that was not a request." The woman turned Terry's head upwards as she pried open his mouth and black smoke funneled its way into Terry. Terry, unable to do anything, could not stop what was happening. In that moment, he had finally woken up from his slumber, no this was a being of pure evil and intent.

Chapter 3

The Man with the Hex

Alex ran out of the cave in a flash with the book in one hand and Liv in the other. Terror, unlike any he had felt before coursed through his veins as he trekked through the barely visible path that he and Liv had just gone through. Behind them he could hear the scuffling of leaves and twigs, it sounded as though an army was coming after them. Along with the sound of the undead screeches and roars, Alex could also hear Tank screaming as he ran with Alex and Liv. He was running just as close as Liv was, Alex could have sworn he heard the big bad badass Hank the Tank whimper as he sprinted through the woods in terror. As they ran Liv was breathing heavily, she was practically hyperventilating as they ran for their lives. Alex was too, he could not believe what was happening, he had seen a lot in the past few days, but he had never seen anything like this before. Looking back on it now, Alex was right to be afraid of what the book could do. As they approached the edge of the forest Alex heard a loud scream come from Liv who had now stopped cold. Alex screamed as well at what he was seeing. Liv's ankle was gripped by a decomposed child. It roared as its nails tore into Liv's ankle.

"AHHHH!!!! GET IT OFF GET IT OFF!!!" Liv screamed. Alex did not know what to do, he looked ahead and saw that Tank was still running away.

"TANK YOU BASTARD!!!!" Alex shouted, he had to act quickly. Part of him wanted to swat the creature with the book but that was exactly what it wanted. He looked around and saw a large stick. With his free hand, Alex grabbed the stick and slammed it overtop the zombie's head. With that, the creature loosened its grip just enough for Liv to kick it off completely.

Liv grabbed Alex once again and they ran. Or at least tried to Liv was limping as fast as he could. Alex knew that they would not be able to outrun them this way. Alex quickly picked up Liv as if he were a groom carrying his bride across the threshold and continued to run. Surprisingly Liv was not as heavy as Alex thought, though he was filled with adrenaline, so his strength was tripled. Not only was his strength higher than it was but so was his speed. Alex sprinted through the woods as fast as the wind could take him. As he was carrying Liv, he had her hold the book as they made their way back.

"You found Eleanor Shrowl's spell book! And used it?" Liv said angrily.

"Is this really the best time to be discussing this?" Alex asked, struggling to find the words to respond while running.

"Umm yes considering that Terry sent the walking dead on us!" Her logic was sound Alex could not keep it in any longer.

"Long story short after my first day of school I found the book and used it to heal myself, then Terry who we then decided to use on Tank but you and I both know if anyone deserves an ass kicking its Tank!" Liv rolled her eyes and shrugged. She knew his logic was a sound like hers. "But then I kept getting these weird dreams about Eleanor Shrowl, she told me to get the book back and when I did—I," Alex did not want to tell Liv about what happened to Mike. If he did, he'd lose her forever. "I never knew the book was capable of something like this."

"Then why did you bring it to the cave?" Liv asked. Before Alex could answer they had finally made it to the main road. Where they heard Tank's truck sputter and chip as he was trying desperately to get the engine to come to life. *That son of a bitch!* Alex thought as he made his way to the car. Before Tank could react, Alex opened the passenger door and plopped Liv in the seat.

"OH NO GET THE FUCK O—" Before Tank could finish a zombie had come in between him and the door. It slammed shut with Alex still on the road.

"Alex!!!" screamed Liv as Tank finally got the engine running.

"YES!!!" he shouted as he reversed out. Before he could think Alex quickly jumped into the tailgate of Tank's truck.

"DRIVE!!!" Alex shouted. Tank immediately slammed his foot on the gas and gunned it. Behind him, Alex had a grand view of the horde of undead corpses. *My god, what have I done?*

***

As fast as Tank drove the horde of undead corpses were slowly gaining on the truck. Panic grew as they approached. Alex knew what they wanted, but he also knew that something far worse would happen if Terry got the book. Or whatever it was that has taken over Terry's body. *Who was that? What was that?* Those questions would have to wait right now, all that mattered was survival. And by the looks of how close the zombies were, and it was not looking so good.

"WHAT THE HELL? GET OFF MY TRUCK!!!" Tank shouted from the driver's seat. Alex could not believe that he was going to leave him like that. Then again part of him was not as surprised considering what he had done.

"Never mind that Tank just keep driving!" Liv said as she held her hurt leg. Alex opened the back window into the front seat to check on Liv.

"How bad is it?" he asked. Just by looking at her leg Alex knew the answer to his question. Her ankle was broken. Alex felt more terrible than he did before he brought Liv to the cave. *She's hurt and it's my fault.* In the backseat of Tank's truck were hunting and fishing supplies along with several boxes of Lonestar beer. This was not his car but his father's. Tank and pressed hard against the gas before long the zombified corpses that Terry had summoned were gone. Alex took this opportunity to get himself a much-deserved drink. He ripped open the box of beer that was in the back and cracked open a can. He had had a beer before, but this felt much stronger than the beer he had tasted. He did not care, after what he had gone through with the mystical beatdown Tank had put him through as well as the trek through the woods with Liv, he above anyone else deserved a nice cold one.

"What the fuck dude!" Tank said when he peaked and saw Alex drinking a beer in the back. "That's my beer you little shit!" Alex could understand his anger but that meant nothing close to the anger he felt towards Tank. Not only did he bludgeon him to a pulp using the book but he took the time and energy to heal him just so he could do it again. *Are you fucking serious right now?* Alex knew for a fact that Tank took joy from the beatdown, which only meant that Tank took joy from every beatdown he dealt. *This guy is a full-blown psychopath!* He thought as he chugged the rest of the beer down. He grabbed another one and handed it to Liv.

"Press that on your leg," he said. She took it without question. Alex looked behind him and saw no signs of anything behind them, not even other cars passing. They were all alone on this road.

"Alex, what the hell was that back there" Tank asked.

"Wow, Tank asking questions before he punches something. There's something I thought I'd never see before" Alex said sarcastically, without hesitation, Tank tried to throw an elbow backwards towards Alex which made the car swerve which also knocked Alex down on his ass. "You dumb sonofa-!!!

"Stop it both of you!" Liv shouted. "Alex fill him in."

"What? No!" Alex said Alex believed that Tank did not deserve an explanation after what he had done to him. If he was not driving, he would toss his ass out of the car.

"Alex please," Liv asked giving Alex her puppy dog eyes. Alex's fury slowly melted when he saw her, and he felt her wish was her command considering she got hurt.

"Fine" he then told Tank everything about how he found the book and how they used it on him at the basketball game.

"YOU MOTHER FUCKER!!! I KNEW IT, I KNEW SOMETHING WAS GOING ON!!!" Tank shouted angrily.

"Will you shut the fuck up! That doesn't matter right now okay what matters is that we keep that book away from Terry" Alex assured.

"Hate to say this babe, but that was not Terry back there," Liv said. Alex knew she was right, the book has him the same book he is holding the same book he tried to destroy. The same book that he unknowingly released an ancient evil that should have stayed hidden where no one would find. Dread filled his body completely Alex could only muster up a single tear in that moment. Alex looked at Liv's ankle and saw that she was still wincing in pain whereas he was completely healed thanks to Tank and his impeccable timing when Terry showed up. The thought came to use the Magik on Liv but something about that seemed wrong to him. *I mean you used Magik on Terry when he got beaten up by Tank what's the harm in using it to heal Liv?* Though he remembered something much like anything else Alex asked Tank if he could help him and that is the same courtesy, he would give Liv.

"Liv do you mind if—" Alex asked while pointing at her leg. She looked and saw what he was suggesting. She nodded and with that, Alex spoke the healing spell which worked as it always had. Surprisingly most people, when they had something as serious as a broken bone, would scream at the feeling of their bones being moved around as if they were marionette puppets. But Liv did not make a sound, she handled it like a champ compared to how Alex did when he did it to himself. And the several other times he has had that spell cast upon him (thanks to Tank). The situation did not improve even after he and Liv were healed, she felt disconnected from Alex. However, who could blame her considering that she had just found out Magik is real in the worst possible way imaginable.

Before Alex could explain himself further there came something over the radio. An old song he recognized from an old cartoon he saw when he was a kid. The song was 'A Man with the Hex' by the Atomic Fireballs. The start of the song was loud, Tank tried to turn off the radio, but the song kept playing even after he turned it off. Alex then felt a large gust of wind behind him. He turned and saw behind him were hordes of zombified corpses chasing after them with incredible speed. But the horde was not alone, along with the horde were several woodland animals with crimson red eyes and foam dripping from their mouths. There were deer, squirrels, rabbits and worst of all a large grizzly bear chasing them with murderous intent. Panic rushed through Alex once more. His arm was covered in goosebumps and his lips became numb. The nightmare was far from over, it had only just begun.

***

"What the fuck?" Tank said as he looked in his rearview mirror. Liv turned around and gasped, she too was horrified by what she was seeing.

"Alex..." she whimpered.

"Tank we've got company!!! Step on it!!!" Tank did as he was told and floored it once more. However, that did not seem to matter as the creatures kept their speed behind them. Alex's mind was racing, he began to look through the back of Tank's truck to see if he could find anything that could be of use to them. He found several more cases of beer and imported vodka. He found a toolbox, a car jack, and a small compartment door on the bottom of the tailgate. "Tank what's in this little hatch?" Alex asked.

"Bessie" He replied.

"What?"

"Just open it dammit!!!" Tank shouted. Alex feared what he would find in there. But he was more scared of what those things would do to him and Liv. He opened the hatch and saw a sawed-off shotgun. It had two rounds already in the chamber. On the handle of the gun the word 'BESSIE' was engraved. *Thank God for rednecks* he thought. Alex had never fired a gun before but if he was to keep Liv alive, he was gonna learn quickly. Alex fired a round into the crowd of zombies chasing after them and missed. The blast of the gun knocked him back down on his butt. A shot of pain went through his shoulder where he was holding the gun.

"Shit!!!" Alex shouted clutching his shoulder.

"Alex hold the gun as tight as you can against your shoulder! Point and shoot!!!" Liv instructed. Before Alex could get back on his feet a large zombie made its way onto the back of the truck. Liv screamed as she saw this creature. It had flowing white hair and red piercing eyes. The right side of its face was completely gone. Alex was able to see its molars from where he lay.

"THAAA BOOOOK!!!" it spoke. Alex scrambled around for the gun, the creature rushed at him once again, and before Alex knew exactly what happened the gun went off. When Alex looked at what he had done he couldn't believe it he blew a hole through the zombie's torso. Alex finally got to his feet and shot once again. This time he did as Liv said and held the gun as tight as he could to his shoulder. And just like in Alex's video game, he was surgical with each shot he took out into the horde. All while 'The Man with the Hex' was blaring in the truck. Tank could not keep the truck steady. There were several times when Alex would fall and lose his footing in the back.

"WOULD YOU DRIVE STRAIGHT!!!" Alex shouted as he reloaded Bessie. Tank was panicking *I guess when you're his size there's really no need to panic* Alex thought. As Alex looked forward, he did not realize it till now but Tank was driving into town. "TANK YOU PYSCHO NOT THE TOWN!!!" Alex yelled as Tank increased his speed. Alex wanted to warn everyone in the town to get inside but Liv beat him to it. Alex had to keep his focus on the monsters that were still pursuing them.

"GET INSIDE! GET INSIDE ALL OF YOU!!!" Liv shouted as they made their way through Main Street. Alex could see that there were several people on the streets shopping as he kept his gun cocked and ready, he did not dare fire another shot, he did not want to hit anyone that wasn't already dead. As they drove on Alex could hear the muffled screams of pedestrians as they too now saw what was coming after them. Alex could still hear that damn song playing from Tank's radio, it felt like he was at a concert due to how loud it was. As Alex sat in the back of the tailgate, he saw the horde attack several pedestrians. One was a cop who had tried firing a few rounds into them but to no avail. There was a homeless couple who tried to climb one of the streetlights but was quickly toppled over by the horde. Several other people including some local farmers were trampled to death by the possessed deer that ran along with the horde. But nothing was more terrifying than seeing a man's head ripped off by the one and only grizzly bear that chased Alex and the rest of them through Main Street.

"Oh my god..." Alex said to himself as he looked out to the carnage that was brought to his town. The town where he had hoped to spend his days with Liv. But now it has become something you would see in your nightmares. And the worst part of it all was that it was all his fault. *If I had never found that damned book none of this would have ever happened.* Dread like no other filled Alex more so than ever. But now was not the time for tears, now was the time for action and if he was to make right by what was happening, he had to do something. Alex swallowed his guilt and began to shoot out into the horde.

***

Five minutes of nonstop violence and carnage reigned on as they pillaged through town then suddenly the truck struck the passenger side. The car jolted to the side but kept moving, Alex was flung almost completely off the truck with that blow. Alex heard a loud scream and the tires screeched through the sound of the music that was still blaring on the stereo. With that blow, Alex also dropped the gun and the book in the tailgate. Alex was now hanging off the driver's side of the truck, he looked behind him and saw more zombies rushing towards him. He let out a loud scream as one zombie tried to rip Alex off the truck.

"AHHHH!!!!"

"ALEX!!!!" Liv screamed. Alex started kicking at the zombie's face but with every kick, he started to lose his grip. Alex looked back at the tailgate, and he saw something finally caught up to the truck. The grizzly bear that he had just seen kill someone. Alex, Liv, and Tank let out a horrifying scream as the bear hopped into the back of the truck making it tilt backward. Alex could hear the tires screeching against the road as the bear made its approach. Though the bear was not interested in Alex or the others, it grabbed the book with its mouth.

"No... NO NO NO!!!" Alex shouted. Alex quickly kicked off the zombie that had his leg and hopped into the back of the tailgate. And without hesitation, he grabbed the book from the bear's mouth. "Oh no you don't!!!" Alex shouted as he tried to get the book back from the bear's iron grip. Meanwhile, more creatures are trying to get close to the truck but are unable to because of the fog the screeching tires were making.

"Alex let it go!!!" Liv shouted from the front seat. Alex refused to let the book go, his grip matched the bear. As he held onto the book the bear whipped and lashed Alex around like a ragdoll. Alex was thrown left and right violently; most people would have let go of the book but for Alex, he knew the stakes and he was filled with nothing but adrenaline. Terror quaked through his mind as he kept his iron grip on the book. But with that terror came a rush, the kind of rush one would feel on a roller-coaster, and if Alex had to describe how it felt being thrown around by the bear it would be how it felt to be on a roller-coaster. Though not one that was a smooth ride, not this one was the one you would steer clear of. Because by the time you got off the ride, you would be sore in places you never thought one could be. Before Alex knew exactly what was happening, he could feel the ground sink beneath him. He was now lifted by the bear which now stood standing tall. Alex refused to let go of the book he was now lifted a good five feet off the ground. He looked directly into the bear's red eyes. It was as though they were made of fire. They swirled and twisted hypnotically. Before Alex could think the bear slammed down on the back of the tailgate with all its weight behind it. Alex felt his newly healed ribs crack once more under the weight of the bear. Alex screamed in pain louder than he ever did before.

"NOOO!" Liv shouted. Alex looked back at the bear which now got to its feet once more, he noticed that the book was no longer in the bear's mouth. Alex looked down and sure enough, he had managed to pry the book out of the bear's mouth. The bear stood tall once more and let out another monstrous roar. Alex screamed once more not in pain but in sheer terror at what he knew was going to happen. But his screams were cut short by the sound of a gunshot. And carefully turned his head backward and looking at the driver's compartment upside down he saw Liv holding Bessie. She cocked the gun once more and shot the bear again, this time square in the face. With that shot fur and brain matter splattered all over the back of the tailgate. The bear fell backward off the truck. Once it did the truck had finally sped forward, and in no time, they had finally made their escape from Main Street.

***

Liv climbed out of the driver's compartment of the truck into the tailgate to tend to Alex. The truck was not moving as fast as it was before thanks to the bear.

"Alex, are you okay?" Liv asked.

"Nice shot" Alex muttered as he lay on the tailgate. She half smiled and grabbed the book out of his hand. She gasped when she saw that the book was damaged not only that, but the ink had become smudged. Alex saw this and sighed. "At least Terry didn't get his hands on it."

"But I can't heal you now."

"I'll be fine, I survived much worse" Alex reassured. Alex felt the right side of his chest, the third rib down was very broken. Luckily it was not pointing inwards towards his lung so that was a good sign. His head began to spin, his eyes began to feel heavy. He could hear Liv's voice as his head slowly drooped down.

"Baby, stay with me—stay—wi-me—" Before he knew it Alex was unconscious once again. And just like before he was back in his own fantasy dreamscape, only this time it was how he left it last time when he saw Terry.

"Terry!" he said to himself in realization. Could Terry be here just like last time? *Only one way to find out.* Just like before he had landed in the middle of a dense forest, only this time there were no leaves, not the trees around him looked dead and rotted as if a wildfire had gone through here. As he ran through the forest it began to feel warmer as if he had stepped into a sauna. Alex was still wearing the clothes he had once when he passed out, he wasted no time in ditching his jacket as he ran through the woods in search of his friend. As he ran, he had this feeling that he was not alone in this forest, no someone else was with him. He stopped and looked around, he turned and saw a teenage girl with long brown hair and brown eyes. She was wearing old clothes. Clothes one would see on the Discovery Channel, there was no doubt who this person was.

"Eleanor Shrowl?" Alex asked. The girl nodded. Alex didn't know whether he wanted to run in the opposite direction or stay put. He had some questions that needed to be answered. "Why are you doing this? Why Terry! What have we done to you?" he asked hysterically.

"I am not the one behind this," Eleanor stated bluntly.

"Bullshit!!!" Alex shouted as he got closer. "Because of that damned book, my town is being torn to shreds! People are dying all because of you!!! And for what? Because I used your book?" There was a silence Eleanor was lost for words. "SAY SOMETHING!!!"

"I am not the cause of any of this Alex... you were when you tried to destroy the book," Eleanor muttered. Alex took a few steps back he was taken aback by what she had said.

"What are you talking about?" Alex asked. Eleanor sighed and walked past Alex. He walked next to her as they walked through this dead forest.

"When you tried to destroy the book, you unleashed someone, someone I had put my life on to remain trapped inside that book."

"Who are they?" Alex asked.

"You already know who she is and now that she's free she will not stop until she has her book and unleashes her army."

"What do you mean I already know who they are? And um, hate to break it to you Ellie, but she already unleashed her army."

"NO!" She shouted. "No... she has merely possessed the corpses of those who had once been people in my town." The realization started to hit Alex. *All those zombies wore clothes just like she's wearing.*

"But what about the animals? Because I was just attacked by a fucking bear!"

"It doesn't take much effort to have animals do what you want but the more she is attached to her host the more powerful she becomes."

"Her host?"

"Your friend" Eleanor answered. Horror stuck Alex once again as he spoke.

"Terry? But why Terry?"

"When your friend used the book, he used one of the spells that she uses on her enemies. Whenever I used the book never would have dared use those spells."

"What do you mean? What makes those spells so bad?"

"The woman you are up against has mastered the darkest Magik imaginable when your friend used that spell, he gave she had chosen who to use as her conduit of evil."

"You mean to tell me that if I had used any of those spells I could have ended up like Terry?" Alex asked hoping he would not get an answer. Eleanor nodded, and with that, Alex knew then and there that all of this was his fault. If he had not shown Terry, the book he wouldn't have used that spell. And if he had not tried to destroy the book, he wouldn't have released whatever was inside the book. Alex stopped in his tracks and tears streaked down his face with this horrifying realization. Eleanor held his hands; her hands were warm and comforting which is strange considering the last time he had seen Eleanor was when she was a zombified corpse.

"Alex, no one is at fault here. Don't you dare blame yourself"

"It is I should have never found that book!" Alex exclaimed. "Oh Terry..." Alex went down to his knees and sobbed more. Eleanor comforted him as he had his breakdown. "I must save him... I HAVE TO!!!"

"I'm sorry your friend is gone," Eleanor said grimly. Alex quickly got back to his feet.

"No... I don't buy that there must be a way to save him there has to be Eleanor please help me save my friend!" There was silence. Alex knew that she was holding something back.

"There is a way to save him, but it will come with a terrible price," Eleanor said.

"Whatever it is, I'll pay it!" Alex said defiantly.

"You will need two things... first you will need the box you found with the book."

"What's in it?" Alex asked.

"Something that will help you" she replied "Then you will need the sword. The sword is the key to salvation for your friend, but if you choose to save your friend you will doom your world."

"What? Why?"

"If your friend gets a hold of the book, he will unleash hell upon your world the sword is the only way to destroy it forever."

"So, what you're saying is I have to choose whether to save my friend or the world?" Alex said.

"Yes, go now Alex Host, and may God be with you for whichever you choose the price will be steep. I ask only are you willing to pay it?" Eleanor asked. Alex looked at her once more as she slowly disappeared. The dreamscape around him started to crumble. The trees splintered and crashed down all around him, and he could hear distant screaming of what Alex was led to assume was people. He turned around and saw the main street once more, only this time there was nothing left but abandoned shops and cars, but also bodies riddled over the main road. One of which he saw was Liv who was ripped in two along with Alex's parents and Flora who was still being held by her mother. *Is this what Terry could do?* He looked ahead and saw a figure floating it was Terry who still looked as evil as he did back in the cave. Alex could never forget how black his skin was and how it somehow looked like smoldering wood as if fire crackled through his face as though it was blood in his veins.

"GIVE ME THE BOOK!!!!!" Terry screamed in an almost deafening voice. Alex stood there in horror he knew he couldn't run all he could do was stand there petrified in fear. Terry then lunged at Alex with fury and Alex shielded his face as he approached.

"NOOO!!!!" Alex shouted.

"Baby, wake up! Wake up!!!" Liv said. Alex opened his eyes, and he was back on the tailgate of Tank's truck" Alex had to reorient himself to where he was when he did he took a deep breath which sent a wave of pain right to his broken ribs.

"Where are we?" Alex asked.

"The safest place we can be right now" Liv reassured. Alex looked around and saw that they were at the high school. Across the front entrance doors was a banner that had HOMECOMING etched across it in a magical font. Alex had a sudden memory of the vision he had when he tried to destroy the book. How people were screaming their heads off and people were being attacked by the horde of zombified pilgrims that they had just escaped from. The voice of the shroud of smoke rang through Alex's mind like a bell. *Your future... oh god no...*

No... no NOOOO!!!!!" Alex shouted as the truck broke down in front of the school.

Chapter 4

Homecoming

Tank's truck was now completely totaled. Alex was not surprised; he could not fight what was happening right now. He was too weak and disoriented to do hardly anything. Liv managed to get him off the truck and she helped him into the school, her arm still holding Bessie. They did not let go of the book as they made their way in through the side entrance. The hall was dark they could hear the muffled party music in the gym. Not only that but Alex could hear people talking, classmates and teachers all conversing, having a good time. Not knowing what horrors lie outside following them. *Why the fuck would they possibly want to be here? Of all the places to go, this was their first thought for a safe house considering how there's a goddamn party going on!!!*

"Why are we here?" Alex muttered. Liv held him and calmly said.

"This was the closest place where we could find medical supplies for you hun." Liv helped him walk to the nurse's office. He heard Liv shuffled around the nurse's desk; she came back a few seconds later with some bandages. Liv carefully sat Alex up on the bed. "Lift up your arms," Liv asked. Alex carefully raised his arms and there were small shots of pain in his biceps as he did so. *Definitely pulled something in both arms.* Liv carefully removed Alex's shirt and jacket. His chest as well as the rest of his torso and back were covered in scratches and gashes from their escape. Some of which Alex could not remember getting because of how quickly it all happened. It seemed only a few minutes ago that he and Liv were back in the cave sharing a tender kiss. Liv wrapped bandages around Alex's chest where the bear's large paw had landed on him.

"Not like I care where he is but where's Tank?" Alex asked. Liv did not respond she was fixated on wrapping up Alex and tending to his wounds. There was this weird tension between them, more so than there was when Alex got her out of the woods. Something was wrong, the question is what? "Liv," Alex said while gracefully touching her cheek. Just as soon as he contacted her skin she pulled away. A part of Alex was both shocked and not surprised by her reaction. If they were to survive whatever this was Alex wondered if he and Liv would still be together. "Are you—"

"I'm fine" Liv responded as though she was being interrogated. Alex's fears seemed to ring truer in her demeanor, she was terrified of him, and for good reason. Just after Liv had spoken Tank busted in the door which made both Alex and Liv jump. Liv immediately grabbed Bessie as Tank entered the room.

"I checked the entrances, no sign of the walking dead," he said.

"Good"

"If we survive this twerp, you are gonna replace my gaddamn truck!" Tank demanded.

"Are you serious? Your worried about your fucking truck? How about the fact that we are being hunted by zombies!" Alex snapped back.

"You mean the zombies that your queer friend summoned?"

"Oh, like you're so innocent! You drove right into town knowing those things were after us! And you didn't care those people are dead! And you don't care!

"I look out for me! And as for those people, it sucks to be them right now!"

"You son of a-!"

"ENOUGH!!!" Liv shouted. Both Tank and Alex were dead silent as she looked as though she was ready to shoot both. "It doesn't matter right now, what matters is that we keep those things away. SO, BOTH OF YOU STOP ACTING LIKE YOUR FIVE YEARS OLD OR SO HELP ME" she shouted while cocking the Bessie. Alex didn't dare make a sound, she looked serious in her intent. Tank looked more scared of Liv than he was of the zombies. Which Alex found mildly amusing. "Tank guard the exits"

"But I—" he said before Liv pointed Bessie directly at his face. He gulped and without breaking eye contact slowly walked out of the nurse's office and into the hallway. Liv lowered the gun when he was out of sight. When she did, she got down to her knees and cried. Alex didn't know how to comfort her; he knew that she was terrified. He was too, but he could only imagine how Liv was feeling at that moment. He did not care if she backed away Liv needed someone and right now the only thing Alex could do was just be by her side as she sobbed. "I'm sorry," Liv said through her tears.

"No Liv I'm sorry, all of this is my fault," Alex said. "I should have never brought you into that cave and I should have never found this damn book," he said while throwing the book across the room. There was a brief silence that filled the room.

"Full discloser I wouldn't have shot you" Liv assured. Alex chuckled and they locked eyes for a couple of seconds Liv's eyes were glassy, still filled with tears.

"I probably deserve it after what I just put you through" Liv smiled and nodded.

"No offense, but this has got to be the worst first date ever."

"Yep..." Alex agreed. The silence returned in the room but this time it was coupled with the sound of muffled slow dance music coming from the gym. "I'll tell you one thing, that was the original plan for our first date," he said while pointing down the hall. With that said Liv got up on the bed and sat next to Alex.

"Oh?"

"Yeah, I was gonna get you flowers, I didn't know which ones were probably roses. I was gonna take you to the dance have a good time then maybe afterward take you back to that canyon what was it you called it?"

"The gates to heaven" Liv replied. They locked eyes once more and her mood slightly improved the more Alex spoke.

"Right, the gates to heaven, I was gonna watch the stars with you" she smiled. It was the first smile Alex had seen since they were at the cave. "It's stupid I know—I'm not good at dates."

"That would have been wonderful" Liv reassured.

"Yeah, it would have—" Alex said while trying to place his hand on Liv's. Which quickly darted away when he touched her. "Liv? Are you afraid of me?" Alex asked.

"What no! You saved my life, it's just—"

"Just what?" Just as Alex asked his question Liv began to sob once more. *She is hiding something* Alex knew there was something else that was bothering her. "Liv whatever it is you can tell me."

"Alex I—" Before Liv could finish her sentence, they both heard distant screaming coming from the gym. Alex and Liv quickly got to their feet and looked out in the halls. Down the hall, they saw a horde of zombies banging at the doors. Tank ran up to them panting as though he had run a marathon.

"Your pals found us dickweed" he said hoarsely.

***

Aside from Tank's arrogant remark he was right they were made. Alex went back into the nurse's office and grabbed the book. Which with closer inspection was worse than he thought. When he ripped it out of the bear's mouth, he had nearly ripped the book in half. The binding had large teeth marks all around both the front and back cover. The pages inside were soaked in drool. And worst of all, the ink of the pages was smudged. Thankfully not all of it was destroyed, Alex still was able to clearly see a few spells he had used. *But will that be enough?* He thought, as he inspected the book out in the hall, he heard more screams. Alex quickly grabbed the book and checked outside. Just outside the school was a cloud of fog covering the ground. It looked as though they were on a cloud by how thick it was. Through that fog, Alex saw an army of glowing red eyes piercing through the fog like how a lighthouse signals on coming ships to shore. And just like those ships, the horrors outside were slowly approaching.

Alex got his shirt back on and he and Liv made their way to the gym where everyone else was. Aside from the dire situation they found themselves in the gym and looked beautiful. There were blue and white streamers draped in stripes along the ceiling. In the corner, there was a white picket fence archway with fake leaves laid out beautifully. *For pictures I assume.* He would have loved to have gotten a picture of her and Liv here. Balloons covered the floor as well as several circle tables with white tablecloths and in the center of all of these tables were bundles of blue roses and candles. Electronic candles, the cheap ones you would find at a party store. Above them was a disco ball that scattered light all over the room in a beautiful array of shining dazzlement though it only made navigating through the crowd of people that more difficult. People were panicking and for good reason, they didn't know what was going on.

"What's happening?" one of the girls said while looking out of the window. "What's going on?" another person asked.

"Are we going to die?" With that said many of the girls in the crowd started to tear up. Some clutched their dates as they did so. Alex could see even the guys were worried about this.

"Nobody is going to die! Okay? We just need to stay away from the doors until help arrives" said one of the chaperones. Alex overheard Tank's voice out of the rest he heard. He looked over and saw him talking to his friend.

"Will, where's my dad?" Tank asked.

"Dude as soon as your dad saw those things, he made a run for it in his car… he left us!" Will said grimly. *Coward*, Alex thought as his arm was tugged by Liv.

"Alex look!" she said pointing just outside the gym into the cafeteria. Colin was there waving him over to him. Without question, Alex and Liv made their way over to him without drawing too much attention to themselves.

"Colin, what are you doing here?" Alex asked.

"Kid, I'm a janitor at a high school dance, you think I came for the punch?" he answered. Alex should have pieced that one together then again, his head was still recovering from his last fight. "Now, how long have you had that?" he asked while pointing at the book. Alex was astonished to know that Colin knew what the book was. His eyes bulged with this realization as well as Liv's.

"You knew that I—"

"I had my suspicions about it after your miraculous recovery the day we met, but my suspicions were finally realized when I saw you yesterday leaving the school." Alex once again could have pieced that together but that did not answer the question he had for Colin.

"Wait time out you know what this is?" Alex asked.

"The Shrowl Witches book yes, I know what it is. Now tell me what you did?" Alex then proceeded to tell Colin everything that had happened since yesterday. Minus the part about what the book did to Mike. Alex still did not want Liv to know, considering all that had happened already Alex did not want her to look at him differently. He then went on to tell him about what happened to Terry. How something or someone was controlling him. "Do you have any idea who it could be?" Colin asked. Alex thought back to what Eleanor said in his vision when he asked her. *You already know who she is.* What did she mean? Though he knew that it wasn't Eleanor, no this was something else entirely something much, much darker. Alex shook his head so he could not think of who or what could possibly be taking control of Terry's body. Colin sighed, "Okay... Liv honey I need you to make your way into the gym locker" Colin reached into his pocket and pulled out some keys and selected one for her. "Use this key to get in, once inside grab the baseball bats and any other equipment you could find in there. Can you do that for me?"

"On it," Liv said as she ran through the cafeteria back into the gym. As she left a sense of worry struck Alex. For he knew exactly what could happen and he knew that he was the only one who could stop what was about to happen.

"Right, now that she is out of the room why don't you tell me exactly what happened," Colin confessed.

"Excuse me?"

"Oh, come on after your last tussle with Tank I called up your mom last night to check in on you and she told me that you, your dad, and your sister were in the hospital. And I'm guessing it had something to do with that" he said while pointing at the book. Alex could not escape it, he had to tell Colin what happened last night.

"After I left the school my parent's boss poisoned my sister and when I finally called him out on it, we got into a fight both me and my dad and..."

"And what?"

"And I killed him, or the book killed him... the guy's head got fried right in front of me..." Alex confessed. There was a silence between the two Alex started to have tears roll down his face just at the thought of what happened to Flora and what he did to Mike. Then he felt a comforting arm wrap around his shoulder.

"Kid, that wasn't your fault, and as far as I tell you were protecting your family. The book killed that prick, not you" Colin assured.

"But I was the one who unleashed that thing from the book and now it's got Terry and oh god the things it showed me..." Alex whimpered.

"What did it show you?" Colin asked. Alex had to think back to what he had seen. The clearest thing he remembered was the sight of the horde of zombies rampaging through the gym. He also remembered seeing Eleanor Shrowl and a burning village as well as a tall old man getting stabbed through the heart by a hooded figure. Not only that but Alex also remembered seeing the countless bodies of children dead by what he could only assume was yellow fever. Alex began to break down the vision Eleanor gave him to Colin. He explained the oncoming attack at the gym and the visions he had of the past. "Is that all?" Alex felt it might help them both if he told him of his latest vision with Eleanor. *Might as well spill the beans on that as well.*

"Just before I came here, I had another vision this time it was of Eleanor she told me that there was a way I could save Terry."

"How?"

"I don't exactly know but she said to find a box and a sword" Colin's eyes bulged wider than Alex had ever seen before.

"What did the box look like?" Colin asked.

"What? What are you—" Colin pulled Alex close he looked fascinated by the idea of this box"?

"Was it small? Had a goat on the front of it two doors on the side kinda looks like a small wardrobe?" Colin accurately described the box that Alex had found when he found the book. Alex was now puzzled yet somehow scared by his reaction.

"Ye-yes how do you—"

"And the sword was it silver?" Colin asked. It was as though Colin was reading his mind. Alex couldn't decide if he was amazed or concerned by how much Colin was piecing together. Before Alex could press Colin further about his abundant knowledge of Eleanor Shrowl Liv came back panting.

"Liv, what's going on?"

"It's Tank he's talking everyone into sending you outside."

***

Alex was not surprised of course Tank wants to take the easy way out. As he entered the gymnasium Alex passed the people who just yesterday were cheering him on as he walked out of the school like a veteran were now met by cold glares. Then again with Tank, he could have made him out to look like

Hitler to these people. I mean their night was ruined but that was not Alex's fault. That was Tank's fault for taking both him and Liv here. If anyone was at fault here it was definitely Tank.

As Alex entered the main dance floor Tank was in the middle of the crowd shouting at the top of his lungs.

"HE BROUGHT THIS UPON US! I SAW HIM SUMMON THOSE THINGS! HE TRIED TO SACRIFICE MY GIRLFRIEND!!! Before he could say another word. A shot was fired. The entire gymnasium screamed and ducked down. The only people who were still standing up were Alex, Liv, Colin, and Tank.

"You lying sack of shit!!!" Alex shouted.

"YOU, SEE? HE'S GOING TO GET US ALL KILLED UNLESS WE DO SOMETHING!!!" Tank exclaimed. Alex had some planned-out speech already in mind for this moment. But Liv had beat him to the punch. She cocked the gun once more and aimed it directly at Tank again. Alex had never seen her so hostile before, which scared Alex more than what was waiting to get them outside.

"You shut the fuck up, you evil bastard!"

"YOU SEE THEY'RE FUCKING CRAZY! AND UNLESS WE GET RID OF THEM THOSE THINGS WILL GET INSIDE!!! Tank pleaded. Liv moved closer to him with the gun which was now directly against his temple.

"If anyone deserves to go out there it's you!" Liv hissed. Alex was now more scared that she was going to shoot him. He did agree with Liv if anyone deserved to be eaten alive by zombies it was Tank, however, it killed Alex to admit this, but they needed Tank if they were to survive.

"Liv," Alex said gingerly. He then moved closer to her and gently placed his hand on the barrel of the gun and slowly lowered it. Alex then looked into her eyes, which were filled with tears. When the gun was fully lowered down Liv collapsed into Alex's arms crying. Alex looked at her and then he looked at Tank. He stood there thinking that he was hot shit, somehow, he was not alarmed by the fact that he just had a gun to his head. Alex grabbed the gun out of Liv's hand and gave it to Colin. "Watch him, don't let him out of your sight" He and Liv walked out of the gym and back into the locker rooms. Liv's wail echoed off the walls of the room as she clutched Alex's arms and shoulders. "Liv what was that back there?" Liv pulled away and wiped the tears off her face.

"Back in the cave—when Tank knocked you out, he—he—" she sobbed once more.

"What did he do to you?" Alex asked. Liv took a deep breath and answered.

"He wanted to teach me a lesson for leaving him—he hit me—and he just kept going and going—" she sobbed once more Alex's mind was fuming with fury and rage. More rage than he had ever felt before. The last time he was this angry was when he went to it with Mike. Alex in a furious dash immediately left the locker room and marched back into the gym where he saw Colin still clutching the gun peering outside. He went up to Tank and before he could Tank could get a word in Alex socked him across the face as hard as he could.

"You evil son of a—" Tank tried to land a punch back, but Alex quickly dodged it and struck him again on the other side of his face. "YOU HURT HER!!!" Alex shouted as he landed three more punches in Tank's gut. Finally, Tank landed a punch across Alex's face. Normally a punch from Tank would knock the lights out of Alex. But Tank did not put all his strength into that punch and Alex was able to brush it off and continue his attack on Tank. He could hear Colin behind him coming towards him. Before he got too close Alex shouted.

"NO! He's mine..." Alex tackled Tank like a linebacker and continued to rain down more and more punches across

Tank's face. Nobody else in the crowd interrupted this fight because of how violent it got. In the heat of this chaos, Alex heard a distant voice behind him.

"ALEX STOP!!!" Alex looked behind him and there stood Liv with tears in her eyes. She stood there and shook her head telling him what he told her 'He's not worth it'. Out of nowhere Alex was flung off Tank's body and slammed down hard against the floor.

"Fun time is over... now it's time to teach you both a lesson!!!" Tank shouted menacingly. As soon as he rushed towards him Alex raised his hand and closed his eyes. He then heard a scream slowly go distant and several gasps. Alex opened his eyes and looked forward. Tank had been flung backward across the entire gym. The entire gym was silent once again. Alex looked at his hand and then back at Liv. *Holy shit!* Tank slowly got to his feet and pointed at Alex.

"Witch..." he said. Then slowly the crowd around them began to say it.

"Witch! Witch! Witch!" Alex gulped as the crowd slowly swarmed him like a pack of lions hunting a gazelle. Before they converged on Alex, they heard a large crash from the gym doors. Right after that crash, the DJ box that sat in the corner of the gym made a piercing screech throughout the gym. Everyone in the gym covered their ears because of how loud it was. Then in a low tone, a familiar tune came through. Just like in Tank's truck the song 'The Man with the Hex' blared through the gym as the banging on the doors became more frequent. Alex quickly turned around and grabbed Liv. Everyone was now looking at the gym doors as they banged and crashed down. *Oh god, they're inside!!!* As the undead entered the screaming began.

***

Piercing screams bellowed through the gymnasium as Alex's vision was coming to life right before his eyes. Chaos ensued, people trampling over each other clawing and running for their lives. Alex, in the midst of this, held onto Liv with all his might. He was not about to leave her side, not while this was going on. The student body rushed out into the hallway and proceeded to enter the closest classrooms available. Alex looked behind them and saw that many people were being trampled upon by other students. One of which he saw was a school staff member. Alex's mind was in a haze of panic, his only goal was to get him and Liv to safety. Through the sounds of people screaming and the roars of the undead horde chasing them Alex heard gunshots. Rapidly firing gunshots. He looked behind him and Alex saw Colin unloading rounds into the pack of zombies on their tail.

"Move!!!" he shouted as he fired into the horde several more times. By this point, Alex had finally made it out of the gym and into the hallway. He could see that people were still flying into the unlocked classrooms. The closest room that he could see was the principal's office, he took Liv's wrist and burst through the door. He looked out into the hallway and saw Colin was still putting up a fight.

"Colin get in!!!" Alex shouted. Colin fired one more round into the horde and bellyflopped into the office. Where he, Alex, and Liv struggled to close the door of the oncoming horde that was trying to claw their way through. Thankfully the principal's room and every other room in the school has a bolt at the bottom of every door in case intruders were to try and break in. Alex quickly bolted the door down and the three of them backed away. The door continued to bang and shutter, but it was holding the horde at bay.

"Good thinking," Colin said.

"Thanks, now what?" Alex asked. There was a momentary silence between the three of them. Alex did not have a plan, that door was not going to last for much longer, and he and the others knew that.

"You need to get back home and find that box!" Colin spoke in a serious tone.

"Box? What box?" Liv asked.

"There's no time to explain! Alex, get you, her, and that book back home, and get that box! You said so yourself that Eleanor Shrowl told you to find it."

"Yeah, so what?"

"So go find that box!" Alex took Colin's words in and realized now that was the only thing that he could do that might stop this nightmare. But he did not know how that tiny little box could ever help them.

"Okay, but how? We don't have a way out of here." Alex prosed. Colin responded by reaching into his pocket and pulling out a set of keys. He then glanced over at the window that was on the other side of the office.

"Take my car and get the hell out of here."

"But—what about you?" Liv asked. There was a silence, the three of them knew exactly what Colin was asking them to do. *No...* Alex thought.

"No—no I am not leaving you here Colin" Alex quavered.

"Alex—"

"NO! No nobody else dies tonight, not because of me..." Colin gently placed his hands on Alex's shoulders. And looked deeply into his eyes.

"Alex, you are the only one who can save us, not me, not her, YOU!" Alex knew that Colin was right. "It's up to you now Alex, save us, save her" Colin added. Alex looked back at Liv, and she looked at Alex with hopeful eyes. Alex looked back at the book. The book that started this nightmare, the book that could release hell on earth. Alex gulped and took a long deep breath. He then thought about his family, and the life he could still have here in Shrowl. He also thought about what would happen if he were to fail. The vision he saw before he woke up when he arrived at the school. The mere thought of the countless bodies that were scattered to pieces throughout the streets and the buildings around the town were splattered in blood and chunks of human flesh. He also thought about

Terry and the kind of hell he must be going through right now. It was Alex's fault for bringing Terry into this mess and it is now up to him to not only save him but also save the world from the fury of the book.

"Okay, okay" Alex muttered as he hugged Colin. The door pounded once louder than it did before. It was now or never.

"Go…" Colin said grimly. Liv grabbed Alex's wrist and moved him closer to the window.

"Alex we've got to go—come on!"

"Thank you, Colin," Alex said with tears streaking his face. Liv managed to get out of the office and Alex quickly followed. The last thing Alex heard from Colin was him shouting.

"GIVE EM' HELL ALEX HOST!!!"

***

Liv and Alex carefully made their way into the parking lot and found Colin's truck. They both hopped inside and started the engine. As soon as the engine started Alex heard something coming from the school. He and Liv looked and saw the horde coming at them again like before. And just like before the radio quickly changed from the classic country station that it was on to 'The Man with the Hex'.

"Oh shit!" Alex shouted as he slammed down the gas and drove out of the parking lot. Alex's mind was racing once again. Adrenaline pumped through his veins as he raced down the main street. The quickest way back to his house. Alex's eyes were glued to the road. There was no chance in hell he was gonna run into anything that might pop up in the road. With what was at stake he was more focused than he ever was in his entire life. Alex could hear the horde gaining on them behind them despite the music that was blaring in the car. But they didn't have any more ammunition, all they could do was outrun them. In his rearview mirror, Alex saw that one of many zombies chasing after they had managed to get onto the tailgate. Its eyes glowed as it crawled its way up to them. Lex gripped the emergency brake and looked at Liv.

"Hang on," he said as he pulled the emergency brake and spun the wheel as far right as he could. Which sent the car spiraling like a top for a solid five seconds. As soon as it stopped Alex released the brake and slammed his foot on the gas pedal. He looked behind him and the zombie that was in the tailgate was gone, whipped off by the spin move Alex had done.

"Where did you learn to do that?" Liv asked.

"Grand theft auto" Alex replied slyly. She smiled as they proceeded to make their way into town. As they made their approach Alex could see that there was not much left of the town when they first went through. The small village of Shrowl had been glistening with red and blue lights. The police were scattered on each side of the road and were helping anyone they could. Alex looked in horror as the town's businesses were destroyed and people were being wheeled into ambulances. He could not help but shed a tear at the fact that all of this was because of him. Then the thought of the vision he had been shown popped into his mind. The vision of what the town would look like if he were to fail at destroying the evil from within the book. The countless dead bodies lay littered throughout the street, plastering the walls and road in blood and carnage. Then a thought came to him, something that he had been told a long time ago by his father.

The time for tears is over, now it's time to get angry. He had told Alex that the day that he got into a car accident was just when he was studying for his permit. It wasn't entirely his fault (much like this situation) but he still blamed himself and his dad told him over and over again that it wasn't his fault. That sometimes people make mistakes and that is okay. That we are not perfect by any means and that it is okay to shed those tears of sorrow. But shed them in only a moment because that's when you need to get angry and fight to make up for what happened regardless of whether it was your fault or not. And that is exactly what Alex intends to do.

As dreadful as the sight of the town was Alex could not cruise through here long. There's no telling how far off the horde is from them if they were to have any chance of saving everyone and everything they needed to get back to the house and find that box.

"Alex?" Liv asked.

"Yes?"

"Colin said that we needed to find a box what did he mean?" Alex proceeded to tell Liv everything regarding the visions he had seen, he felt that if there was ever a good time to come clean it might as well be now. He told her about the vision he had from homecoming, and what Eleanor Shrowl told him to do. "A box and a sword? The same sword the paster had back in 1670?"

"Yeah"

"And just how the hell are we supposed to find it it's been missing for over three hundred years" Alex could not answer because frankly he had no clue, but he knew that if he didn't find it Terry's soul would be doomed.

"We have to find it or else the rest of the world will suffer."

"But who could be doing this? You said that Eleanor told you to get the book and the sword?"

"Yes, it's the only way to save Terry and the rest of the town" Alex answered.

"Alex, how do you know it's not Eleanor that is destroying the town?" Liv asked.

"Because she told me."

"And you believe her?" Liv responded. Alex could not answer.

***

They were now less than half a mile out from Alex's house. The rest of the way was backroads and gravel roads.

Which made Alex very concerned. Just moments ago, before they reached the town, they were being chased down by a practical army of the dead. But now, now it feels quiet, way too quiet. The radio had finally cut off that ridiculous song, though now Alex kind of wished it was back on. The only thing he could hear out there was the sound of crickets. Chirping throughout the night, finding their way home, much like how Alex was.

"ALEX WATCH OUT!!!" Liv shouted. Without warning the driver's side door of the truck was shoved inwards by something. The impact of the collision sent the car onto its side. Thankfully Alex and Liv were wearing their seatbelts when it happened. Alex's head was splitting open by the impact he looked down at the passenger seat and saw Liv was still conscious.

"You, okay?"

"Yeah, what the hell was that?" Alex carefully released his seat belt and climbed out from the top and saw that it was a large buck deer that was tattered and deformed. He then heard something just down the road. Growls and grunts, creeping closer and closer.

"We gotta go now!!!" Alex shouted as he reached the truck. Both Liv and Alex managed to hop out of the car and saw exactly the source of those noises. Sure enough, it was the horde from the school. They also saw the deer that had run into them slowly crawl towards them. It started making these strange honking noises. It almost sounded as though it was still gasping for air. Without question, both Alex and Liv made a run for it. Alex still had hold of the book while Liv had hold of the still-empty shotgun. In the distance, Alex was finally able to see his house. He took Liv by the hand and they both raced down the long driveway of Coven Road and into the house. Alex quickly grabbed his dad's reading chair that he had in the living room and propped it up against the front door. He looked back in the living room and thought back to the night before when Mike had died just a few feet away from him. He had to push the memory back once more, he had a mission and that was to get the box.

"Liv stay here I'm gonna get the box," Alex said as he made his way up to his room. He slammed open his door and investigated his closet and just as he left it the box was there. He gazed at it once more, this silly little box that looked like a small wardrobe but what could possibly be inside that could help him in his most desperate hour? Before Alex could open the box, he heard a scream coming from downstairs. "LIV!!!" He stuffed the box in his jacket pocket and ran back downstairs and saw an almost empty living room. There was someone in there, someone familiar to him.

"Oh, so nice of you to join us, Alex," said this person in almost a growl-like voice. Alex took a few steps closer as it finally turned around. It was Terry or whatever it was that was possessing Terry. Alex now had a better view of his face. Which now resembled blackened burnt chipped wood. There were patches of white mixed into it like the kind you would see in a bonfire. His skin had cracks coming from every corner of his face. And in between those cracks, you could see veins of fire and brimstone as if there was still a little bit of fire brewing inside of Terry himself.

"What have you done to Liv?" Alex asked the creature. Without saying anything Terry lifted his hand and Liv levitated towards him along with his parents and Flora. Their mouths were gagged, and his dad looked as though he had been through another beating. He had dried streaks of blood streaming down the sides of his face. Along with bruises and swelling across the left side of his face. Alex's mother had streaks of mascara across her face. She still had tears swelling in her eyes. Flora was shaking like a chihuahua, she too had tears in her eyes as well. Unbridled rage swelled back into Alex's heart. All he wanted to do at this point was to pounce on Terry (or whatever was possessing Terry) and beat the hell out of him. "YOU SON OF A BITCH!!!"

"Give me what I want, and I'll let them go," Terry said. Alex looked at the book and back at Terry he knew what he could do with the book, but he also knew that he would kill his family and Liv without question.

"Who are you?" Alex demanded.

"Didn't poor lil Ellie does not tell you?" He spoke. "Tsk Tsk, you already know and the answer to that question is right in your hand." Alex looked and saw that the only thing he had in his hand was the book. Terry raised his hand slightly and with a flick of his wrist the book exploded and landed on one singular page. The first page Alex saw.

This book is the property of Morganna Starr

The shock sent chills all over his body. How could he not have figured this out sooner? Terry is possessed by the original owner of the spell book.

"You—your—Morganna Starr?" Terry smiled menacingly and laughed.

Chapter 5

Morganna Starr

How could I have been so stupid Alex thought. He stared into the cold black eyes of the person who was once his friend. Who had now been transformed into the very person who created the book. Alex could not believe it; Ellie told him the truth it wasn't her causing all this chaos. It was Morganna.

"Surprised?" Terry said now in a dark womanish tone. It reminded Alex of the raspy voice of an old woman who had been smoking for twenty years. The one you would see with a gaping hole in their neck on TV. "Bravo Mr. Host you finally pieced it together! It only took you a week!"

"It was you..." Alex murmured. There was silence in the room. Alex looked at Terry who smiled menacingly. "You were the thing I saw come out of the book; you were the one that put those images in your head!"

"And was I right?" Morganna responded. Alex stood there in silence. "Alex you and I are not that different," she added.

"How so?"

"We're both killers. Sure, body count might be a little off, I've killed plenty of people but you—you have so much potential!!!"

"I have never killed anyone, and I never will!"

"Are you sure? Think about where you are right now. What happened right before your eyes!" Morganna added.

Alex investigated the living room and the image of Mike's limp corpse lingered in Alex's mind. He could still see the stained wood from his blood on the floor. Alex remembered the loud crash of the light as it engulfed Mike's head. How it practically swallowed him like a hungry shark swallow its prey. "Look at me Alex," Morganna spoke. Tears began to stroll down his face. He did not want to give her satisfaction. But in the end, he had made his realization, the realization he was avoiding. "I SAID LOOK AT ME!!!" Alex finally did what he was told and looked at Morganna. "You look me in the eye, and you tell me how I could have killed that idiot." Alex remained silent he could not answer. "Don't blame me for his death that was not me, that was you ALL YOU" she said pointing at him. She was now acting as though she was a child who had won a bet. Flamboyant and cocky, almost whimsical in a dark twisted way. Alex looked at Liv and his parents with tears in his eyes. Her words cut deep deeper than anything that had ever been said to him. Alex did not know exactly how to handle this shocking truth. He saw that his parents as well as Liv and Flora all had tears and fear in their eyes.

"I didn't mean to—I—swear he was going to—"

"Yeah, yeah yeah blah blah blah MURDER IS STILL MURDER KIDDO!!!"

"Shut up"

"How did it feel? After my first kill, I felt as though I was reborn!

"I said shut up Alex demanded.

"Oh, wait a better question how did it look? Oh, come on! You have got to tell me you practically had a front-row seat tell me did his skull explode like confetti or—"

"SHUT THE FUCK UP!!!!" Alex made a charge at him and was immediately knocked down again by Morganna. Who looked as though she had barely put in her full strength. With that blow, Alex had dropped the book onto the floor. Alex saw this and leaped for the book but just before he could touch it, he was beginning to feel stiffness all over his body, he felt this feeling. He tried to move his arm, which was half an inch away from the book. He could not even move a finger. Alex's body was then flung to the ceiling. Alex felt like a fly trapped in sticky tape, he could not move all he could do was watch as Morganna grabbed the book and held it gently in her hands like a mother holding a newborn.

"There you are my precious, it's okay did the mean man hurt you?" She said as though it could talk, she then held her ear to the book. She then gasped and looked up at Alex. "He did, oh Alex your naughty boy you used my book on cheap jokes. Ha! You have no idea the kind of power you possessed, and you squandered that power just so you could get—" She then looked at Liv and smiled. "—a girl, though I have to say Alex you know how to pick them she is quite a beauty. She'll look great as a parlor maid don't you think?" Liv's entire face was now covered in tears as Morganna stroked her face as if she were a cat.

"You stay away from her!!!" Alex shouted. Morganna looked back up at Alex and smiled once again.

"Hate to break it to you Alex but you are in no position to negotiate, if that was an option, to begin with." Alex tried to wiggle his way through the enchantment. He felt something in his jacket pocket start to shuffle. He wiggled once again and just as he did something fell out onto the floor. It was the box, the box that Eleanor Shrowl had told him to find. The one piece of salvation against the witch was now right in front of her. She stared at the box for a couple of seconds, she looked puzzled. She picked it up and held it up against Alex's face.

"What do we have here?" Morganna spoke sarcastically. "Where did you find this little trinket?" Alex was silent, she knew he knew what it was. "TELL ME BOY!!!" she screamed. The screams sent the house shaking by how intense it was.

Alex could hear the muffled screams of his parents and Liv. Tears dripped off Alex's face as he too was scared shitless. His lips and face were numb, the rest of his body felt empty and hollow like a log. But at that moment, he thought back to what Colin told him when he left the school.

'Give 'em hell' *Damn right* he thought. He took a deep breath and spoke to Morganna with confidence.

"You seriously don't know where you're standing, do you? What this house is who it belonged to. This is the home of the one woman on this Earth that can destroy you! The woman you convinced me was evil. But that's not the case, she is not the evil one in this story, it's you. It has always been you since the day I found the book! You wanna know what that box is it's a gift."

"Is it now?" Morganna said pondering it some more. She looked up at Alex and smiled. Without hesitation, Morganna slammed the box against the floor and it splintered into a million pieces.

"NO!!!!" Alex shouted. What was inside the box was a small grey stone. Morganna picked it up and held it against Alex's face.

"This is what the great Shrowl Witch sends her champion? A rock? Hahahahaha!!!!"

***

Alex could not believe what had just happened. Eleanor's secret weapon for saving Terry is a rock. *What could that do against Morganna?* She laughed hysterically for almost a minute. She could not believe it either.

"That is priceless!!! A rock? Oh, sweet Ellie, this is the best you can do?" she chucked the rock behind her and proceeded to speak. "Normally I would just kill you Alex, but I do love it when the light leaves the eyes of a child when its life is snuffed out."

"DON'T YOU DARE TAKE ME!!!" Alex shouted. Both Alex's parents tried to wiggle out they too were shouting and screaming but whatever control Morganna had on them was muffling their voices, as well as Liv's. Flora's screams were muffled as Morganna dragged her by the hood of her onesie.

"After I am done with her, I will kill you mother then your father let this be a lesson for you Mr. Host that Magik always comes with a price!" In Morganna's free hand was a crimson red and black ball of fire. Alex continued screaming and squirming trying to break free of Morganna's control until suddenly he stopped, he looked behind Morganna and saw the rock she had tossed behind her. It began to glow blue and teal. The light from the stone started to grow brighter and brighter. The room was now engulfed in cool blue light. On the floor where the stone was blue fog rolled across the room towards Morganna and Flora. Alex looked at Morganna and from the looks of her (or from Terry's face) she looked concerned. Morganna took a few steps backward and she and the rest of the people watched as the blue fog slowly crept over Flora covering her like a cloud blanket. It practically swallowed her whole. All that was seen was her silhouette being projected by the blue light cascading above them. The light then grew brighter and brighter once more until it became so bright that everyone including Morganna had to shield their eyes.

"What is going on? What have you done boy!" Morganna shouted. Alex could not answer because he did not even know what was happening. But something about this comforted him and made him feel as though there was still hope. In what felt like an hour of pure blinding light the light from the stone slowly dimmed and the fog receded into the stone. The fog had revealed Flora who was still in her original state. Her eyes were closed but not gripped tightly in fear like how they were when Morganna grabbed her. She looked more like she was sleeping and standing up.

"What—" Morganna said before she was cut off. Flora gracefully waved her arm up and snapped her fingers. In that instance, Alex, Liv, and his parents were freed from whatever dark Magik that was binding them. The four of them huddled together and looked at Flora awestruck.

"Flora?" Alex asked.

"Honey, what's happening?" Libby asked. Flora slowly opened her eyes and instead of seeing her deep brown eyes, they were now bright blue.

"Nice to finally meet you face to face Alex" Flora said without lisping and in a more adult voice. Alex recognized that voice he had heard that voice before in his visions. The visions Eleanor Shrowl had shown him. The realization hit Alex like a truck. He could not believe what he was seeing *it couldn't be...*

"Eleanor? Eleanor Shrowl?" Alex asked. Flora smiled and nodded.

***

Alex could not believe what he was seeing it was her (granted it was in the form of Flora) but it was really her, the Shrowl Witch herself. *That's what she meant by there was something that would help you in the box, but I never thought it would be her inside. But wait, that would mean that she has been inside that box the entire time.* The voices he had heard in his room at night, all came from the box in the closet!

"Impossible..." Morganna spoke hesitantly Flora (or Eleanor speaking through Flora) looked at her in triumph.

"What's the matter Morganna? You look like you've seen a ghost." Morganna rose quickly and her hands began to engulf in flames once again. She smiled menacingly and spoke once again.

"This must be my lucky day I get to kill you again!"

"You forget one thing Morganna, I sealed you in that book before and I am going to do it again!" Eleanor shouted.

"You think that I am afraid of a child you're more of a child now than you were when I found you in that pond! I mean look at you at least I chose someone slightly more threatening than you" Eleanor smiled and flinched in Morganna's direction which caused her to flinch as well.

"And yet you are here you are a grown woman afraid of what a little child could do to you" Eleanor giggled. Her eyes glowed that same light the stone gave off as she started to levitate off the ground. Her mouth opened and the light bursted out of her like sunlight shining through an open doorway. When she did that Morganna cringed and squealed. Alex looked at her and saw that the rough bark-like skin that was Terry's was now being burned off Morganna. Alex could now see patches of Terry screaming in pain. *My god whatever happens to Morganna surely that would mean that Terry's getting hurt as well.*

"STOP! You'll kill Terry!!!" Alex shouted. Eleanor did not listen she was not letting up for a second. Before Alex could act Morganna leaped out of the line of fire and grabbed Liv.

"Seeing as you damaged this body, I guess yours will have to do darling," Morganna said smiling. Before Alex could get another word out Morganna and Liv disappeared. The last thing Alex heard before they left was the sound of Liv's scream.

***

"NOOO!!!!" Alex shouted as he ran out the front door. When he looked outside, he saw that the horde of undead corpses that had chased him for the past couple of hours were all gone. But the skies were still red and black. This was far from over and Alex knew he had to get Liv back and save Terry.

"Alex hun are you okay?" Libby asked her son. He walked right past her not answering. Alex marched into the living room where Eleanor was admiring the new body she had just possessed.

"I will say this was not what I had in mind, but I guess desperate times call for desperate measures." Eleanor chuckled.

"I'm sorry what part of this is funny? A fucking witch who is currently possessing my best friend just took my girlfriend hostage and you're in here complaining about the body you possessed. Who just so happens to be my baby sister and I swear to God if anything happens to her, I will fucking exorcise you!" There was silence in the house Eleanor could see on Alex's face that he was not kidding. She sighed and spoke once again.

"You're right, forgive me when you've been stuck inside a box for four hundred years you tend to forget your manners."

"Sorry not to butt into your conversation here but what the hell is going on?" Donald Host shouted.

"Long story short the Shrowl Witch is real, Terry got possessed, I got chased by zombies and the world might be ending because I found her spell book in my room when we moved here does that about sum it up?"

"Umm did you mention the part where you used the book on your tormentor?" Eleanor added.

"WHAT?" Donald shouted.

"Look it doesn't matter now, what does matter is that we stop Morganna and end this madness before she can finish the ritual," Eleanor explained.

"Ritual? What ritual and when you say stop Morganna what exactly do you mean?"

"Alex, I told you already your friend is gone and if Morganna is looking to possess your lover she will have her the only way to destroy Morganna is to destroy her host as well" Alex's heart dropped when she spoke his hands began to feel numb once again. *No... no no no no no*

"You lied to me!!!" Alex shouted.

"The only way they can be saved is if the spirit allows itself to leave that's why when this is all over, I will happily return your sister to you" Alex could not comprehend what he was hearing this was all too much. He angrily kicked his backpack across the room and screamed. His mother comforted him as best she could.

"It'll be okay hun," she said in his ear. He shook his head and responded.

"No... Mom, you don't understand I love Liv. I'm the reason she got taken if I hadn't taken her to the cave to try and find that stupid treasure so that we could stay here none of this wouldn't have happened."

"What do you mean so we'd stay here?" she asked.

"Dad said that we'd be moving since he lost his job," Alex replied.

"Oh, honey I didn't know you wanted to stay."

"Well, I do, I wanna stay with Liv!" Alex exclaimed.

"Tell you what sweetheart when this is over, we'll talk about living arrangements okay?" Alex looked at his mother with tears in his eyes and he hugged her tightly.

"Miss Shrowl, you said something about a ritual what ritual are you talking about?" Donald asked.

"I don't have time to explain." She spoke.

"Then make time dammit because our world depends on it!" Alex shouted. Eleanor sighed and held out her hands to Alex.

"Fine, it's only fair that everything is explained." Alex grabbed her hands and then Eleanor took a deep breath in and slowly the world around them started to fade to black.

"Eleanor, what are you doing?" Alex asked.

"I'm showing you the rest of my story, the real story the story. The one that nobody talks about."

"Why?"

"Because this is the story of how Morganna Starr nearly destroyed everything and everyone."

***

In an instant Alex was no longer in his house he was in the woods, it was dark. He looked around and realized that he was now completely alone in the woods. Eleanor had vanished, the only thing that Alex was able to see was a man leaving a small wooden cabin.

"Hello? Excuse me sir" Alex asked. The man did not answer, nor did he notice Alex was there at all. He looked around once more to see if he could find Eleanor but then he heard her voice in the distance. He looked back at the cabin, and he heard her voice coming from inside. Alex moved in closer to see what was going on peered in through the window and pressed his hands against the glass. He could see Eleanor and another woman fighting. And in Eleanor's hands was the book. Alex's eyes focused more on the window he was looking through and he saw that his fingers had gone through the glass. He pulled away and looked at his hands, they were completely fine. He took his hand and pressed it against the window and his hand shifted through the window entirely. It was like entering a room through one of those beaded doorways people used to have in the seventies. *Well, if it's safe for my hand to go through I guess the rest of me would be safe right?* He carefully walked right through the wall and entered the cabin.

The cabin itself was very well furnished considering the timeframe which to Alex's mind he could only guess that this was the 1600s when Eleanor Shrowl was still alive. The cabin had a nice fireplace and next to it was a pile of wood and a rocking chair. He looked back at Eleanor and the other woman they both were sitting at a kitchen table. Alex moved closer to Eleanor and saw that she had just recently been crying.

"Ellie, what did you do? You knew the risk and yet you still did it! You just had to use that godforsaken book!" the woman shouted.

"Greta... I thought I—"

"NO, YOU WEREN'T THINKING THOSE KIDS DIED AND THEY SHOULD HAVE STAYED DEAD BUT YOU JUST HAD TO PLAY GOD!!!" Greta retorted. Eleanor quickly got out of her chair and got up in Greta's face.

"You sound like the Pastor, mind your tongue."

"HOW DARE YOU!!! I am nothing like that monster! You know just before I came after you and Jacob, he was rounding people up? He went to everyone's houses and brought them to the church to testify."

"Testify what?"

"Witchcraft," Greta said grimly.

***

Alex's body went numb as he witnessed history unfolding before his eyes. He had heard stories of what happened to the men women and children across the state of Massachusetts who were accused of witchcraft. How the Puritans tortured them into confessing. There was one method of "interrogation" that terrified Alex the most. He remembered his teacher calling this method the boulder test. Unlike dunking the accused witch into a pond or lake, in this method, the accused would be strapped to a rock and would have a large boulder on their chest. If they did not confess their torturers would have another boulder and another until either they confessed, or their rib cage collapsed completely. When Alex was told that he could only imagine how that would look like and now seeing this he might actually see it in person.

Alex looked at Eleanor, her eyes now looked glassy. Alex could tell that she looked devastated by this news. He did not know the full context of what had just happened, but he could gather that Eleanor felt like she was to blame. Before she had time to fully process what Greta had said she rushed over to the kitchen table and opened the book once again.

"Ellie, what are you doing?" Greta asked, Eleanor did not respond she was fixated on the book. "Eleanor gives me the book," just like before she did not respond. Greta then tried to pull the book away from her, but Eleanor gripped it tightly. "Give me the book Ellie."

"No…"

"Give me the goddamn book!"

"NOOO" Eleanor shouted as she pounced onto Greta, they both rolled around the floor kicking and clawing at each other. Alex had always wanted to see a chick fight before but the fight that he was seeing now horrified him. *I think I'm better off not seeing a chick fight again Jesus* he thought. Greta finally managed to pry the book out of Eleanor's hand, she then took a couple of steps backward.

"This book has done too much Ellie! And you want to play God again?" Greta pleaded.

"I have to try and fix this!" Eleanor sobbed.

"Just like how you fixed those children that we killed using this book!!!"

"I did not know."

"No, you did not care!!!" Greta shouted. Greta then moved into the living room and looked directly at the fireplace.

"Greta, what are you doing?" Eleanor asked.

"I'm sending this book right back where it belongs. IN HELL!!!" Greta shouted as she hurled the book into the fire.

Eleanor screamed "NOOOO!!!!" As she leaped towards the fireplace just as she did, Greta held her back and whispered in her ear telling her that it was alright. "Do you realize what you have done? You've doomed us all!!!"

"Ellie..." Greta said coldly.

"Without that book, those children's souls are doomed, and the village will be slaughtered!!!"

"Ellie..." she repeated.

"What are we to do now Greta? Tell me! TELL ME!!!"

"ELEANOR!!!" Greta shouted. She then pointed at the fireplace. Eleanor turned her head and saw that the book was not burning it looked to be in the same condition as it always has been. As Eleanor moved closer to the fireplace. She began to hear a chipping sound. This sound grew louder and louder, and it seemed to be coming from the fireplace. She then saw exactly what was causing this sound the stones that the fireplace was made of began to shift and turn slowly. As they shifted the fire died out and in its place was a large purple and blueish light emanating from the fireplace. Alex could not believe what he was seeing, and he knew Eleanor and Greta were feeling the same way. There was wind coming through this light, it seemed to be sucking everything into it. Eleanor looked down at the fireplace and saw that the book had just been sucked into this light.

"NO!!!" She said as she raced into the light without thinking.

"Eleanor wait!!!" Greta shouted as she followed behind her. Alex had to see where this story would take him so just like Greta, he followed them into the unknown.

***

Alex passed through what he could only describe as a hallway of light and stars. It looked as though he was traveling at lightspeed like they did in Star Wars. He followed Eleanor and Greta through this mysterious path not knowing what could be on the other side. Then again, knowing that this is what really happened to Eleanor Alex did not expect it to be good. Through his own experience with Magik, he had never seen anything like this before whoever did this must have studied for years, decades even. And Alex had a pretty good idea of who could have done this.

After about five minutes of walking through this tunnel of light, the three of them arrived on the other side. They were now in a different house entirely. The furniture in this house was much nicer than the cabin they were just in. Overhead Alex saw a chandelier made from deer antlers. This house was much more spacious than the one they were in, and it looked to have been built fairly recently. It had a certain smell to it that made Alex think of apple cider. Whoever lived here must have been rich for this time.

"Ellie... does this house look a little familiar to you?" Greta asked hesitantly. She glanced over at Eleanor and saw that she was now looking out of a large window overlooking a hill with a dead tree at the top of it. Alex followed her to the window and gasped at what he saw. Outside Alex could hear muffled screams of people in the village. He looked outside and saw that there were two houses on fire and kids running around with their eyes glowing emerald, green. Eleanor saw this and tears trickled down her face.

"This is Pastor Flease's house..." Eleanor responded. Both stood there stone-silent for a couple of seconds, Alex saw the fear in both of their eyes as they made this startling revelation. Alex tried to remember what he could about the pastor but the only thing that came to mind was that vision he had received from Morganna when he released her from the book. One thing that he did remember was the sword that was used to kill him and the fact that the person who did kill him was shrouded. For all Alex knew it could still be Eleanor who killed him.

"We must leave right now!" Eleanor exclaimed, both she and Greta made their way to the fireplace where they had just come from but before they could the fireplace exploded into a raging fire that blocked their path. Although Alex could not be seen, nor could he interfere with what was happening even though he was scared out of his mind. Behind him he heard a familiar voice, laughing as she approached the fireplace. Alex turned to the source of the laughter and there she stood in the flesh Morganna Starr. Who he did not expect to be so beautiful for a woman in her mid-thirties. She was slender, and poised and had a long black cloak wrapped around her. Her eyes were like sapphires, and her complexion (much like the rest of her) was also very slender and narrow. She was also carrying a large bag behind her. Alex could not see what was inside, but something told him it wasn't anything good.

"Delilah? What are you doing here?" Eleanor asked. Alex looked at her curiously. *Delilah?* He thought as the scene played itself out.

"Ellie, you know this woman?" Greta asked.

"She was the lady that owns that cabin, she was the first person I saw after I came out of the pond where I—" She paused and looked at the fireplace then back at Morganna. Who stood there smirking menacingly.

"Where you died... and where you found my book. Tell me sweet Eleanor what secrets did you find inside?" Eleanor looked at the book then flipped to the cover and saw who the book belonged to.

"Allow me to introduce myself, my name is Morganna Starr, and if you would be so kind as to hand over my book"

***

Alex could not help but compare the exact expression Eleanor gave Morganna to his own when he found out the truth. The only difference he could make between Eleanor's reaction to his was that she felt more hurt by this realization. Alex's reaction was pure terror and confusion.

"It was you—you were the one who brought me back it was you who left your book there for me to find!" Eleanor shouted.

"Yes, it was though I did not give you my book no no no. See when I did bring you back, I did not want to be spotted so I ran. I had only just enough time to finish the spell when I ran my book fell out of my cloak."

"But why? Why bring me back?"

"I have no time for this squabble" Morganna answered. Eleanor quickly made her way to the fireplace and held the book over it.

"Answer me!" There was silence in the room, everyone in the room knew that the book could not be burned. But Eleanor's threat seemed to be enough for Morganna.

"Very well I shall humor you" Morganna slowly paced her way to the large window and began to share what only Alex could describe as her life story.

"I was born several villages away, my mother bless her soul died when she gave me life. My father's grief saw no end, he thought that he could remedy it with rum. He had told me about my mother and how she used to love animals. Sadly, under my father's care, those animals' lives were lost. As the years went by my father later resented me. Said that I was the reason my mother was not here and anytime I spoke of her I was met with the backside of his hand!"

"Every night I prayed that I could just hear her voice and every night I was met with nothing but silence. But then on the night of my eighteenth birthday, I finally heard someone calling. But it was not my mother, no it was my master the very one who made that book you have there Eleanor."

"Your master?" Eleanor interrupted.

"Yes, my dear, Lord Rednaxela, he told me that if I did his bidding, I would be able to see my dear mother again. Not only that but he also told me things, secret things that would make even the bravest men cower in the face of my power. He told me that I could not only see my mother again but that I could also have a new family and with that family, we could become queens! But for that to happen I needed to grow my power and so I did until I was ready." She then sat the large bag down on the floor and opened it. Inside was silver and gold. "What would a queen be without riches for me to flaunt" she added.

"But what do I have to do with me?" Eleanor asked.

"Well don't take this the wrong way dear but you were a test."

"A TEST!!!!"

"Yes, you see, I needed to know that I was strong enough to carry out my master's plan and I am and all I need now is that book and—" Before Morganna could finish her story the doors of the house opened, and in came Pastor Flease and several other villagers. One of them had brought in a torch, from what Alex could tell either they had come back here to regroup, or they saw the fire coming from outside. Although Alex could not be seen or hurt by what was happening, he was terrified by what could happen here.

"What the hell?" Pastor Flease said as he investigated his home. Eleanor and the Pastor locked eyes and in those mere seconds of eye contact, it felt (to Alex) hours had gone by. There was obvious tension between the two of them.

"Oh my god, it's—it's you..." he muttered.

"It's the witch!!!" said one of the villagers. Just as he spoke three of the villagers broke apart and grabbed Eleanor, Greta, and Morganna. Eleanor and the Pastor did not break eye contact as she spoke to him.

"Hi Pastor, it's been a while how's your daughter? You know the woman who killed me!!!" Eleanor shouted.

"As far as I am concerned child, she cleansed our town of your wicked filth! And now you've come back to induct more gullible people to pursue Satan's path!" There was a small silence in the room that was quickly broken by the sound of laughter. Both the pastor and Eleanor looked over at Morganna who sneered menacingly.

"Satan wishes he had this kind of power..." she muttered. She then waved her arms and the fire from the fireplace burst out into the living room and engulfed two of the villagers into walking fireballs. The house echoed their screams as the remaining villager was crushed and skewered by the antler chandelier. Upon looking at this grim sight Alex threw up, after he did, he continued to watch more.

"Thank god nobody saw that..." he said to himself. When he looked back at the carnage, he saw that the man who was killed by the chandelier had dropped his torch, Alex looked at Morganna, and with a soft blow, the fire started to spread. She then looked at the Pastor who now stood at a defensive stance.

"Stay back demon!" he shouted as he slashed away with his holy silver blade. Morganna simply chuckled once more, she flicked her wrist and in an instant, the sword was now in her hand. The Pastor both astonished and terrified of what just occurred stared at the woman as she observed his blade.

"Hmm this should do nicely," she said as she rushed towards the Pastor and thrust the sword through his stomach. The pastor gasped for air as the sword slowly slipped out from his body. He fell to the floor hard, Morganna left the sword in the poor man's corpse which now stood out like a messed-up monument to Morganna's wraith. As Alex looked around the house the fire was spreading fast, and Eleanor and Greta were now on separate sides of the main living room area. He could see the fear in their eyes as they looked at Morganna. At that moment Alex felt that exact fear as well. Not for this version of Morganna but for the one he knows he must face in the present.

Alex looked upon Morganna and instead of seeing the living version he had seen only moments ago he now viewed her as she looked in his time. Black, decayed, deformed, and teaming with evil.

"Ellie, my sweet, sweet Ellie, you could join me," she said. Alex looked back at Eleanor and her eyes looked hesitant. "Together you and I could find your family, WE could be a family! Think about it, Eleanor, you could not only have your family back, but you could also have Jacob all to yourself! All you must do is give me the book!" she demanded.

"Don't listen to her Ellie she is lying!" Greta said through the fire. Just as she said that Morganna raised her arm and in an instant Greta was thrust into the air gasping for air as she was being strangled.

"DON'T LISTEN TO HER!!! YOU COULD HAVE EVERYTHING YOU EVER WANTED AND MORE!!!" Morganna shouted.

"Don't hurt her!!! Please don't hurt her I'll give you the book if you let her go..." Eleanor pleaded. Morganna smiled and lowered her arm and as she did, so Greta was released from her grasp. Both Greta and Alex said to themselves 'no' as Eleanor walked over to Morganna and handed her the book.

Morganna now had the book in her hands and at last proceeded to flip through the pages chuckling as she did so and in an instant, Eleanor pulled the sword out from the Pastor's body and thrusted it through Morganna's back. At that moment everything was coming together for Alex, Eleanor in a final act of defiance killed Morganna just before she could perform her master's grand scheme. Morganna choked on her blood as she clutched the book in her hands. Which Eleanor easily snatched away from her. Morganna looked upon her killer as she stared down at her in triumph.

"Goodbye, Morganna..." Eleanor said, fire erupted all over the house in an instant the entire living room was engulfed in flames.

"Ellie come on!" Greta shouted from across the room. She and she were separated by a wall of fire. Eleanor looked at the book in her hands and then back at Greta. Alex did not know what could happen at this point. Above everything else that he had seen, he wanted Eleanor to go to Greta. But instead, she turned away and fled with the book in her arms.

"ELLIE—ELEANOR!!!" Greta shouted. There was another burst of flames that sent her running outside to the rest to the man that Alex saw coming from the cabin earlier. Alex then chased after Eleanor as she ran not only with the book but the money Morganna took with her as well as the pastor's sword. Eleanor looked out upon the hill of her village and saw that it was in ruin. Alex could see in her eyes that she blamed herself for what had happened. *If only she could hear me, if she did, I'd tell her—*"

"That it wasn't my fault?" Eleanor asked now, looking directly at Alex. Confused Alex stood there not knowing if she was speaking to him. "Yes, Alex, I can see you," Alex looked out into the village and saw the carnage that unfolded. Not only did the children that Eleanor brought back make it to the village, but the people were panicking like animals. The screams of those people in the village echoed throughout the valley.

"There is still one final chapter in this story," Eleanor said just before the village slowly dissipated into smoke. He was now in a cottage and Eleanor looked much older than she had been before. She had to be in her mid-twenties at this point. This cottage looked familiar to him. Almost too familiar. As he looked around, he realized where he was now.

"Oh my god—" he said to himself. He was now inside his house once again, or rather in this case Eleanor's house when she lived here. Outside he heard the commotion of villagers shouting and hollering. All of them saying 'burn the witch' and 'burn in hell'. In a panic, Eleanor grabbed the book and rushed upstairs to the first door on the right and placed the book into a familiar cubby. She then reached into her pocket and pulled out the stone that was in the box and whispered to it. Alex could not make out any of the words because it was of a language that he had never heard of.

"That stone was one that I picked up at the pond where Morganna brought me back" she explained. When she was finished, she placed the stone inside the box and closed the cubby.

Eleanor took a deep breath and slowly walked down the stairs and out to the front door, with Alex following behind her.

Chapter 6
The ritual

As he walked out of the front door Alex was met by another bright light. This light was warm and comforting, he moved slowly towards it, and in an instant, he was standing in his living room once again. His parents stared at him with tears in their eyes. Alex did not realize it, but he too had a single tear streak down his face as he came back to reality. His dark, dark reality, the reality that Morganna had come back for revenge and to fulfill her master's plan.

He wiped the tear off and looked down at Flora who was still under Eleanor's influence. He locked eyes with her and in Flora's eyes were tears, tears of sorrow. Alex now understood completely the untold story of Eleanor Shrowl. How she was manipulated into a wicked plan, a plan of world domination by a force greater than anyone had ever seen before. As if the situation wasn't already bad, knowing now exactly what Morganna has in store only made the need to find her and Liv greater. She now had the book, they were doomed. Doomed to face whatever Morganna has to offer.

"Alex? What's wrong honey what happened?" Libby asked her son. There was a silence that filled the room like a thick fog.

"Oh my god—" he groaned. Alex took several steps backward and placed his hand on the fireplace in the middle of the living room. His head was now splitting in two because of what Eleanor showed him.

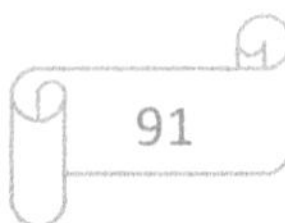

"You understand now? When I said that your friend cannot be saved, I meant it. He cannot be saved" Eleanor said grimly.

"What just happened?" Donald asked.

"I showed him exactly what he needed to see, the story that nobody had been told before—mine" Eleanor responded.

"What did happen to you though?" Libby asked. Eleanor sighed she did not want to answer but she felt as though they deserved an answer.

"After Morganna killed the Pastor his daughter—my murderer dedicated her life to hunting me down and finishing the job and she did with the help of the survivors of the town" Eleanor added.

"She killed you twice?" Alex asked. Eleanor nodded; Alex paced across to the front window. "What about the children you brought back? And Greta?"

"All of those questions will be answered later once the book is safe," Eleanor responded. Alex looked back at Eleanor who at this point was still possessing Flora's body. Which made what he was about to say way more uncomfortable.

"I could give a flying fuck about that damn book! In case you forgot Morganna kidnapped my girlfriend!!!"

"ALEX!!!" Donald shouted. "You need to calm down! That is still your sister. Right?"

Eleanor nodded and answered, "Yes she is fine, right now she thinks she's dreaming, though for some reason she's dreaming of some talking blue dog is that normal?" Alex thought back to how much Flora liked Bluey. It's no surprise that's what she'd dream.

"Heh, yeah that's normal, but she'll be safe with you in the driver's seat?" Libby asked. Eleanor hesitated before answering.

"That I cannot guarantee, we need to find Morganna and that book before she does her ritual" Eleanor responded. There was a small silence that was broken by Alex.

"What ritual? Morganna spoke of it, but she didn't fully explain it with what you showed me." Alex said. There was silence in the room once again. This made Alex's stomach curl part of him did not want to know, if Morganna was going to do it chances are it was not going to be good.

"The ritual of Graada..." Eleanor muttered. Alex looked at his parents and their eyes turned into globes. "It is a dark ritual named after the first Magik user who tried to enact it."

"What happens if she performs this ritual?" Libby asked.

"WE CANNOT ALLOW HER TO PERFORM THE RITUAL!!!!" Eleanor shouted with tears in her eyes. "If she performs that ritual, she will literally open up the gates of hell..." With that said the room felt cold, and Alex felt goosebumps all over his body. His body went numb with shock, the only thing that he could feel was his still beating heart pumping through his chest. Which at this moment felt as though it was going to pump out of his body. *Oh my god...* he thought. Alex's mind was completely blank at this point, the only thing that he could think of was those words "Oh my god".

***

Panic finally struck him like a freight train and Alex went from sheer terror into pure determination. A determination to stop Morganna and end this before it could even begin. If what Eleanor says is true then not only is Liv's life in danger but also the rest of the world.

"I need to find them," Alex muttered as he made his way to the door. Donald stopped him before he could open it and gazed at him.

"You're not going anywhere with that psycho out there, plus you don't even know where they are" he stated.

"Dad, I am the only one in here (who is alive) who has used the book, no offense."

"Mhm," Eleanor grunted. Almost everyone in the room knew that he was right at this moment. Donald did not want to believe his son.

"Alex, it's too dangerous even for you, Morganna has the book what chance do you have?" he muttered. There was a small silence in the room that was broken by Alex who hugged his father tighter than he had ever hugged anyone before. Alex took his time before answering his father's plea, he could hear in his voice the dread and sorrow coming from it.

"Dad, what chance do we all have if Morganna goes through with her plan? It has to be me, Dad, it's me or the world" Alex answered. There was a silence Donald knew this was the only way but his fatherly instincts took hold.

"What if we run?" he pleaded.

"It wouldn't matter dad, let me do this please!" Alex begged. Before his father could answer there was a commotion outside. Libby looked out and gasped.

"What? What is it?" Donald asked.

"It looks like the whole town—oh my god they've got torches" she answered. Overhead the four of them could hear a chant coming from outside. 'BURN THE WITCH, BURN THE WITCH!'

"We must go, they will only hinder us" Eleanor exclaimed. Alex knew that she was right but did not want to leave his family behind. He and his father locked eyes. They both knew now what needed to be done and with no words, they hugged each other as tightly as they both could. For they did not know if this would be their last time embracing or not. Alex kissed his mother on the cheek, and he grabbed Eleanor's (or Flora being possessed by Eleanor) hand and made their way to the back door.

***

The angry mob surrounded the front half of the house. They consisted of farmers and their families. Along with many of the business owners and other town folk. Alex did not realize it until now, but he felt a heaviness in his pocket he reached in and felt a pair of keys. His dad's car keys to be precise. *Guess that hug was more than just a goodbye* he thought. The outside garage was just thirty feet away from the house. Both he and Eleanor snuck their way into the garage without being spotted. Alex unlocked the car and quickly moved Flora's car seat to the front passenger seat.

"What is the meaning of this? And what is this contraption?" Eleanor asked.

"This is a car seat and unless you want to be a red smear on the road you'll shut up and hop in. In case you forgot you're in my sister's body and I am not about to lose her too are we clear?" Alex explained. Eleanor stopped talking and let him buckle her in. Alex started the engine and revved around the crowd. They, being as angry as one could ever possibly be screamed at and cursed at them as they made their escape. The back window of the car was blown out by someone in the crowd who had brought their gun along. In the distance, Alex could hear his father screaming behind them.

"RUN ALEX RUN!!!!"

***

Alex did not know where he was going. Morganna could be anywhere, as far as he knows she could be performing the ritual as he speaks! He was driving blind into darkness that he did not know where to find.

"Eleanor, where could she be you must have some sort of idea where they could be?" Alex pleaded. Eleanor rubbed her head for a few seconds and looked back at Alex.

"Alex, think back and I mean really think for one second—What's the one thing that Morganna wants more than anything?"

"What?"

"Just answer the question" she retorted. Alex's mind only thought of what Morganna was going to do.

"To perform the ritual"

"Wrong—think back! She said the reason she studied Magik and the reason she must perform this ritual is because she thinks the ritual will give her a family!" Alex completely forgot about Morganna's motives. His mind was only focused on what would happen if Morganna performed the ritual.

"Not only that but remember what she said?" Eleanor added. Alex thought for a second time and then the words came to him.

'What would a queen be without riches for me to flaunt' Alex recited. In that instant, Alex knew exactly where Morganna had taken Liv and where she planned on performing the ritual. *The treasure!*

***

Alex whipped the car in around the first right turn he saw and started his journey to the cave once again. *Of course, Morganna would go back to the cave but why did she take Liv?* That was one question that had not been answered by Eleanor. Alex was scared to ask, part of him wanted to know the other did not.

"Eleanor answers me this, why did Morganna take Liv?" There was silence and visible hesitation that struck Eleanor when he spoke. "Eleanor why did Morganna take Liv!" he repeated.

She sighed and answered. "The Ritual of Graada requires a human sacrifice in order for the gates of hell to be open, the death of an innocent must be paid as a prelude to all the other soon-to-be innocent victims around the world" Alex's heart sank once more, part of Alex was not surprised by this realization. The thought of Liv's body being used to unleash hell was haunting. He pushed that thought aside and floored the gas pedal. Before they cut the last turn, they needed to make before they reached the trail something very large hit the car on the driver's side. This collision sent the car crashing into a tree. The collision happened so fast that there was no time for either Alex or Eleanor to scream or react. The airbag deployed and as Alex raised his head it started to split, he got a concussion or two from that crash. *Flora,* he thought (granted he knew at this moment that Flora was not in control of her body he knew he had to be sure she was safe). He tried reaching toward her with his left arm, but he couldn't, it was broken. Alex's vision was blurry, and his ears were ringing before he knew what was happening someone pulled him out of the car and threw him on the ground.

"HOW YOU LIKE THAT BITCH!!!" he heard. Alex didn't need to fully hear this person to know who it was. It was Tank, coming back after him. Alex tried to crawl away with his good arm and Tank immediately stopped on his hand breaking it. Alex screamed in pain and clutched his hand. He then got a swift kick to the gut which sent all the air out of him. Despite the pain he was feeling in this moment his only thought was on Liv and Flora and keeping them safe.

"Ple-a-se st-op" Alex pleaded. Tank laughed menacingly, he dropped down to Alex and spoke very softly.

"Ya know, if I had known that you'd be the cause of all this shit I would have finished you off when I first saw your bitch ass. And now, now, I am doing the lord's work by killin' you. Once you're gone everything will be just fine, and the best part is nobody is gonna care when you are gone" Alex's vision was slowly starting to come back Tank grabbed Alex by the face so that their eyes locked together. "I want you to look at me while you die you motherfucker. I want to see the light go out in them." While his vision was still blurry Alex's eyes did see something inching its way behind Tank. Alex smirked slightly which made Tank furious. "What's so goddamn funny!"

"You're wrong—I'm the one who's going to be the hero, and nobody is gonna remember you," Alex said with triumph.

"And why is—" Before he could finish Tank was pulled back by one of Morganna's undead corpses and thrown backwards. Before he or Alex knew it Tank was surrounded.

"But it does suck that you won't be there to see it," Alex said as he got back up and rushed to the car. He could hear the sound of Tank being torn to pieces by ravenous monsters as he pulled Flora out of her car seat and ran into the forest. His screams echoed through the forest as he ran. Part of Alex felt guilty then again, he felt it was poetic. Tank was a monster, and it took a monster to kill a monster. With that thought in mind the thought of a much more sinister monster that was lurking ahead of him.

Goodbye Tank and hello Morganna Alex thought.

***

The red sky made traversing through the trail almost impossible. Thankfully Alex still had his phone with him, and the flashlight was on. He had to hurry, who knows what could be lurking in this forest. The memory of the horde of zombies that had chased him earlier came through him. He didn't see what they did to Tank, but he could only imagine what happened. The thought of flesh and skin being ripped off him like paper was chilling. That same chill went straight down his spine. He found that his mouth was completely dry as if his body could no longer produce saliva. Alex took that as a sign to run, run far away, and keep Flora (or in this case Eleanor) safe. But he knew in his heart that he couldn't no matter how much he wanted to.

Flora slowly woke up and rubbed her head. She looked around puzzled then back up to Alex.

"What happened?" she asked.

"Trust me you don't wanna know." Alex continued through the trail while still carrying Eleanor in his arms. As he walked through the woods, he could not help but compare the forest to the dream he had had when the skies were as red as they were now. When Eleanor warned him about how to "save" Terry by using the sword and finding the box with the stone inside containing her soul. The last time he was on this path he could not get the sound of crickets out of his ears. As he walked through this time around, he could not hear a thing. The only thing that he could hear was the sound of him breathing heavily and his heartbeat.

"Could you please let me go now" Before Alex could put her down, he heard a crack behind him. It was the crack of a tree branch. Alex looked behind him and saw a large figure following them. It growled and snarled at them as it approached slowly. They heard another branch breaking just off to their right. They turned to look, and another figure appeared out of the shadows of darkness. "On second thought don't put me down" Alex began to run through the forest clutching Eleanor for dear life. As he ran, he could hear footsteps all around him, he felt as though he was a zebra being hunted by a pack of lions in the jungle. And just like a pack of lions if he was caught, he most definitely would be eaten along with Eleanor. Behind them, Eleanor caught a glimpse of what was chasing them. It was (to no surprise) the monsters that had just got done eating Tank though thankfully the zombified animals that chased them through the town were nowhere in sight according to her. Alex leaped over logs and large gaps in the trail he had run faster than he ever had in his life. He could hear the creatures behind him bark, yap, and growl as they tried desperately to ensnare their next meal. The worst part was that Alex was completely defenseless, he did not have Tank's shotgun on him this time nor did he have the book to use either. Their only hope was that he'd be faster than the raptorial monsters chasing after them.

The chase ended when Alex eventually tripped on an overgrown branch, which sent Eleanor flying forward. Before Alex had any time to react, Eleanor was whisked away by three creatures kicking a screaming. As Alex attempted to rescue her, he was struck on the head by a large branch and was out like a light.

***

Alex was now back in the forest from his dream, he could tell it was a dream because of the obvious trail there was laid out before him. The trail to the cave was overgrown and barely visible. This trail looked as though this was paved out by a national park. He walked the path hesitantly he could tell that there was death all around him not just because the skies were crimson red but because, unlike most dreams, he could actually smell death in the air. It was foul and rank and yet somehow burnt and crispy. It's as though someone had barbequed corpses in the wilderness surrounding him. Whatever it was, it made Alex dry heave a couple of times. As he kept walking through the thickness of the forest, he saw several dead squirrels and rabbits on the path. And as he walked further on, he saw more dead animals. Deer, snakes, elks, hell even bears, the more and more he walked on the more he saw death doing its work on the wildlife. It was almost unbearable that is until he came upon a sight, he wished he hadn't. Laid out upon the trail was Liv with a large hole in the middle of her chest where her heart was.

Alex's eyes swelled into tears as he knelt beside her and held her in his arms. His heart shattered at the sight of Liv's lifeless body lying limp in his arms.

"No...no no no no" he muttered as he held her head on his lap. He kissed her forehead and kept apologizing to her. "I'm so so sorry Liv."

"How touching" a voice spoke behind him. Alex quickly turned around and was now facing the woman he had seen in Eleanor's vision of the past. The true face of Morganna Starr. "It's nice to finally meet you face to face Alex."

"Leave her alone..." Alex demanded. Morganna laughed maniacally at his request.

"Oh, Alex your poor insignificant child don't you see? Your precious Olivia is going to be what brings me my master back from his eternal prison she will be honored in years to come for her sacrifice."

"You don't have to do this! Take me instead please just not her!" Alex pleaded. Morganna simply shook her head and replied.

"No, no I don't think so compared to you she's much more pretty of a sacrifice, and well you—to be honest I don't know what she sees in you."

"I know why you're doing this! I know what your master has promised you."

"YOU DON'T KNOW ANYTHING ABOUT ME BOY!!!" Morganna shouted.

"I know that he promised you'd see your mother, not only that but he also promised you a family, right? A family that loves you and treats you with kindness, right?" Morganna was silent as Alex spoke once more. "Morganna, whatever it is that your master has promised you it's a lie, a cruel cruel lie that was devised by someone who only means to bring

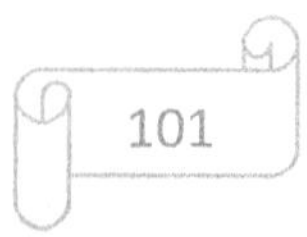

destruction. The only person who could bring him what he wants is a woman who wants nothing more than to feel loved and cherished by her family. And most of all by her mother, the mother she had not met" Morganna could not answer him. "I am begging you Morganna stop this please and I promise you I can find a way for you to be at peace the only one who can stop this madness is you" With that said Alex and Morganna locked eyes they both had intent within them. However, Morganna's mind had been made up for almost three centuries.

"LIAR!!! I AM GOING TO GET EVERYTHING I WANT AND A MERE CHILD IS NOT GOING TO STEP IN THE WAY OF THAT!!!" Morganna screamed as she raised her hand and sent Alex flying backward into a tree. And with that impact, Alex awoke and he was back in the cave.

***

Alex's head was splitting again, a little sense of déjà vu came over him as he looked out into the cave. The last time he was in here he was knocked out by Tank, though right now in this moment he wished it was Tank that he was dealing with. In the cave, he saw a circle of torches around what Alex could only assume was a blood-painted pentagram. In the center was a podium about the size of a twin bed. On it were veins carved into the rock that stretched outward onto the pentagram. He looked around and saw that he had been chained to the ground by his wrists. Part of him wanted to try and escape but knowing that Morganna placed him in these shackles there would be no point.

In the distance, he heard a familiar voice shouting and screaming. He looked in the direction of where it was coming from and sure enough it was Liv being dragged by undead soldiers onto the podium.

"LET ME GO YOU SON'S OF BI—ALEX?" she blurted. They locked their eyes once again. Alex could see the fear in her eyes as he gazed into those sweet majestic blue eyes. He could see that any hope that was there left her body as she saw her knight in shining armor sitting there shackled and defenseless.

"Liv, I'm so sorry..." he muttered. "I should have never opened that damned book I should have never gone to look for that dumb treasure, I should have never involved you," he said through the tears.

"Alex, I don't wanna die..." she said shaking in terror. As those words left her mouth Alex finally tried to shake his hands out of the chains and just as he anticipated it was no use. By this point, Liv was laid out on the podium and was chained by her wrists and ankles. The soldiers ripped open her shirt then proceeded to take their hunting knives and slice horizontally across their arms and paint a pentagram onto Liv's chest. Along with what looks like ancient runes like the ones Alex saw in the book.

"Liv look at me..." Alex demanded, she did as she was told. "If this is it—if this is how it all ends, I just want you to know that I—"

"I love you too" she answered. This tender moment was cut short by the sound of footsteps and laughter.

"Ah love such a weakness don't you agree?" Morganna spoke as she entered the circle.

"LEAVE HER ALONE TAKE ME!!! TAKE ME DAMMIT!!!" Alex shouted. Morganna shushed and raised her hand.

"You should be honored Alex you're about to witness the ascension of a queen and what is a queen without her riches" As the words left her mouth Alex felt something hard hit his head he looked down and saw that it was a silver coin. He looked up and saw that the ceiling was raining down coins and jewelry. *The lost treasure* he thought, as it poured down from above. The cave echoed with the sounds of clinging metal, almost to the point where it was deafening. As bad as this situation is Alex couldn't help but be mesmerized by how the silver and gold twinkled through the cave. Then again most of this was due to the blunt head trauma he had just come out of. Morganna approached the podium and with a snap of her fingers, one of her undead warriors brought with them a goat. Alex remembered seeing in the book the ritual and how in it there had been pictures of goats. Morganna then spoke, but it was in a language that Alex could not make heads or tails of. When she spoke a small spot of the wall behind her began to glow red and it then began to steam. As if there was something molten hot melting through the wall and into the cave. He could smell the melting rock from across the room. When it was done Alex heard a loud clang echo through the room much louder than any of the coins that had fallen. Whatever just fell sounded like there was some real weight to it.

Morganna snapped her fingers once again and another one of her minions brought it to her. Alex could not believe his eyes at what it was. It was the holy silver blade, the same silver blade that Eleanor had shown to him in his visions. The same holy blade that killed Morganna when she was mortal, the same holy blade that could end this eternal nightmare! Her minion brought it to her and delicately placed the sword in her hand. On the other hand, she held the head of the goat that was brought to her.

She looked at Alex and smiled. "Recognize this blade boy?" she asked rhetorically. "This was what your precious Eleanor used to strike me down, and now—now it will bring me the very thing I have waited centuries for" A thought occurred to Alex after she spoke, *where's Eleanor?* He looked around and did not see her, the last thing that he remembered was Eleanor getting taken just before he was knocked out.

"Where's Eleanor? Where's my sister you heartless bitch!" Alex shouted.

"SILENCE!" she yelled; her voice reverberated through the cave like an earthquake sound. Alex was speechless as he stared down Morganna with hate coursing through him like a river. Morganna then raised the sword above her head and chanted.

"TONIGHT IS THE NIGHT MY BROTHERS AND SISTERS!" her voice echoed through the cave as if she was speaking into a megaphone. "TONIGHT, OUR MASTER RETURNS, AND TOGETHER WE TAKE THIS WORLD!!!" her minions began to roar as she began to chant in a language Alex could not recognize. Morganna took the sword and sliced off the goat's head. Blood gushed out from the bottom of the goat's head like a fountain. Morganna nodded to one of her minions who walked over to the podium and held Liv's head still and plugged her nose. Morganna brought the head over her head and forced Liv to drink the blood of the goat.

"LEAVE HER ALONE!!!" Alex shouted. Liv gurgled and choked as the blood went down her throat. Alex struggled more than ever to free himself. He could not bear to see this go on any further. Once the blood had finally stopped dripping out of the goat's head Morganna chucked the head into the darkness of the cave. Liv coughed up blood violently.

"Much like how your god asks you to drink his blood and eat his flesh my offering will drink the blood of the beast that resembles my master, and she will become the flesh he consumes only then will he return to his full strength and together we will rule this world like gods among men!!!" Liv looked back at Alex terrified. Without saying it Alex gave her a look that said *Don't stop looking at me.* Pure horror struck both of them as Morganna began to chant in that unknown language again. When doing this the ceiling of the cave began to change the rock and stalactites crumbled and fell as the ceiling became a red cloudy whirlpool. Inside Alex could hear a distant growl that slowly grew louder and louder. Above them, the room glowed red by the light of two glowing eyes. It was as though the cave had produced its dark evil sun it was so bright. When his eyes finally settled Alex saw Morganna's master.

***

Rednaxela's return to the mortal plain was unlike anything Alex had ever seen before. He expected this creature to come from the ground (given that's where hell is). But instead, he came from the ceiling of the cave. The creature itself resembled a goat-man hybrid. It tried desperately to claw itself out of the portal hole from the ceiling, it was about a quarter of the way through. From what Alex could gather based on Rednaxela's sheer size he had to be at least seventy feet tall and fifty feet wide.

"COME MY MASTER AND FEAST UPON THIS MORTAL AND TOGETHER WE SHALL FEAST UPON THE WORLD!!!" Morganna shouted through the howling winds that overcame the cave. Rednaxela roared coarsely through the cave and with that roar came a scream. Liv's scream, the scream of someone who knows now more than ever that this is their end.

While witnessing this unfold Alex felt a tug from his shirt behind him. Then he heard a whisper in his left ear.

"Don't turn around and hold still" Eleanor said. Alex's eyes bulged, there was still hope, slim hope but hope, nonetheless.

"How did you—" Alex questioned.

"Let's just say this tiny body has its advantages" Eleanor summed up. She then waved her hands at the chains on Alex's wrists evaporated. "Now how are we going to get the book back from Morganna?" Eleanor pondered. Alex looked at her and smirked, a thought came to him. A simple but effective solution was staring him in the face.

"Why are you smiling?" Eleanor asked.

"Well, you said it yourself that tiny body has its advantages, right?" Eleanor looked at him dumbfounded. Alex quickly picked her up and gave her instructions. "I'm gonna chuck you right at Morganna you grab the book and I'll get Liv sound good?"

"What? No! Put me dow—" Before she could finish Alex threw her towards Morganna who was too distracted by the whirling winds and chaos her master's arrival was bringing. Both Eleanor and Morganna collided hard, it brought Morganna backward and caused her to drop the book. Alex looked around and saw that Morganna's minions had fallen over. I guess *they must be linked,* he thought as he rushed over to Liv and untied her from the podium. As this was going on Rednaxela let out an earth-shattering roar which made more and more stalactites fall around them. The walls echoed for miles both inside and outside the cave. And the ground was shaking violently as the mighty beast roared in pain. It didn't take much for Alex to realize that the cave was coming down, they needed to get out now if they were to survive this encounter.

Alex quickly grabbed Eleanor on his way out. She still had the book in her hands as they made their escape. Everything around them was coming down behind them as Alex and Liv ran for their lives towards the night sky.

"COME ON! COME ON!" Alex shouted as they jumped to safety just outside of the cave.

***

Everyone's ears were ringing due to the cave-in, Alex didn't realize it until now, but he was clutching both Liv and Eleanor in his arms.

"You alright?" he asked them both, they nodded, they were safe, safe, and secure at last. Alex let out a sigh of relief and held them tighter in his arms. Liv kissed him graciously as Eleanor slid out of his grasp. Alex looked back towards the cave and couldn't help but feel a sense of overwhelming guilt and sorrow. Morganna was still in Terry's body when the cave went down. Terry was gone, and it was all Alex's fault. Alex's relief was almost instantly replaced with grief and shame.

"Terry... I'm so sorry" he whimpered Liv comforted him as he wept for the loss of his friend. Alex's body was shaking all over and the mixture of pain, shock, and sorrow made this moment above all other painful moments he had experienced in the last few days all the more unbearable.

"He's not suffering anymore Alex, you gave him peace" Liv assured him, this sadly did not help give Alex any sort of comfort. *Oh god, what have I done...*

***

Liv lifted him and began to make their way back home. Before they could embark on that long trek home, they were interrupted by a loud scream. Alex and Liv looked behind them and saw Morganna clutching Eleanor by her hair. Her small body was lifted at least three feet from the ground.

"PUT HER DOWN!!!" Alex demanded.

"You killed the only family I could have had boy! Now I plan on killing yours starting with this little one!!! HAHAHAHA!!!!" Morganna cackled as she brought the holy silver blade closer to Eleanor's throat. Alex quickly grabbed the book off the ground and shouted the one spell he knew how to use properly.

"Kamarro!!" in an instant the silver blade was ripped from Morganna's hand and was flung towards Alex who then caught it with ease.

"DO IT ALEX!!!" Liv shouted.

"KILL HER ALEX!!!" Eleanor added. Both of them screamed at Alex for him to kill his friend the very friend he had thought just moments ago was dead. He then looked at his hand holding the sword and into the other hand which clutched the book. Then a thought came to him, one that he had not considered until now.

"No..." he spoke blankly.

"Coward" Morganna muttered. "What's wrong boy can't bring yourself to do the job yourself?"

"I won't kill my friend" Alex stated as he dropped the book on the ground. "The only one dying tonight is you Morganna" The witche's eyes bulged by what she was witnessing. She quickly dropped Eleanor and thrusted towards Alex.

"NO STOP!!!"

"Go to hell Morganna!" Alex shouted as he stabbed the book with the holy silver blade. With that thrust of the blade, Morganna let out an agonizing cry of pain. Alex plunged the sword deeper into the book and the more it went through the more Morganna suffered. Alex repeatedly stabbed the book with each stab the book produced a whirlwind of red clouds that surrounded both Alex and Morganna. The trees shook violently, and the wind howled and moaned almost as loud as Morganna screamed. He looked at the book which began to bleed black goo which looked to be bubbling as if the black liquid was being boiled. Morganna stood before him clutching the blade opposite him whining in pain.

"This—cannot—be!!!" she muttered. Morgaana's evil exterior slowly transformed back into how she looked when she was alive. Alex gazed upon her one last time as a single tear strolled down her face. As it did her face along with the rest of her body began decomposing right before Alex's eyes.

When Morganna's body evaporated the wind eased, and the tree stopped shaking. Alex looked down and saw that the book was covered in that black ooze that was now dried, it was now properly destroyed. In front of the book were the dusty remains of Morganna Starr. Alex went to his knees and once again let out a sigh of relief, the nightmare was finally over. The book was destroyed and Morganna was gone.

"Alex, are you okay?" Liv asked kneeling to his level. He did not respond, he just kept looking at Morganna's remains. A gust of wind revealed something under the mound of dust and ash. Alex looked and saw that it was an eye.

"Liv—look!" he exclaimed. The mound of ash shifted and slowly rose from the ground. As it did, more and more dust and ash shook off revealing what was inside. Alex could not believe his eyes at what it was. It was Terry alive and well, covered in ash and black soot.

"What the hell happened?" Terry asked hysterically. Alex and Liv rushed over and hugged him tightly. Alex let out a few tears of joy, his friend was safe, and he had finally done something right.

"We'll explain later man we're just happy that you're okay" Behind them Eleanor watched this reunion, Alex gazed over her and silently thanked her. She gleamed at him with pride. She too could not believe that this was now finally over. This tender moment was put on hold by the sound of a tender voice.

"Ellie" Everyone looked around wondering where that voice had come from, and then they heard it again this time louder. "Ellie" behind Eleanor was a bright white light that seemed to be coming from where the cave was. The light was warm and shining so bright that everyone except for Eleanor covered their eyes. Alex could make out several silhouettes in the bright light their shadows provided enough shade for him, Liv, and Terry to see who they were. Alex recognized one of them as Eleanor's friend Greta (the one he saw in the vision). There were other people with her including a tall man and a little boy.

"Peter!" Eleanor exclaimed.

"Miss Shrowl who are they?" Liv asked. She looked back and smiled.

"My family" Eleanor walked up to Alex and smiled. "I suppose I should return your sister to you," As she said that Flora fell right into Alex's arms, and before them was the spirit of Eleanor Shrowl exactly how looked before she had died. She was just as beautiful as Alex saw in his visions. Eleanor smiled and let a couple of tears stroll down her face.

"Thank you, Alex, for returning me to my family. Enjoy the time you have with yours, oh and before I forget" Eleanor raised her hands in the air, her hands glowing the same bright light coming from the cave. When she was done, she put her hands to her side.

"What was that?" Alex asked.

"Consider it your reward, I think after all you have been through it's the least, I can do." Alex smiled and thanked her. "Goodbye Alex Host and thank you for bringing me home" Eleanor walked into the light of the cave and as she did the light slowly disappeared. Alex could not help but feel a little emotional at this point. Pride beamed through him like a warm light, it filled him up through every part of his body. He had helped a three-hundred-year-old spirit find peace.

Alex, Liv, and Terry all stood up and when they did Alex heard a clinging sound coming from his pants pocket, he reached in and saw that his pockets had been filled with silver and gold coins, as well as different colored gems that shined in the light of the moon.

"Oh my god!" Alex exclaimed. Both Liv and Terry gazed upon the treasure in awe. Alex reached into his other pocket and found more and more diamonds and gold inside. All his pockets had been filled with Eleanor Shrowl's stolen treasure. The three of them heard a long yawn, they looked down and saw that Flora had now woken up.

"Alex?"

"Yes?" he replied.

"I had the craziest dream" The three of them laughed hard at that remark. Alex picked up her sister and began to head back home.

"I bet you did Flora, I bet you did"

Chapter 7

The portrait

A week had passed since Alex Host fought back the forces of evil. And through that week of peace came time to heal both physically and emotionally. Alex expected there to be a mob back home when he returned from the battle against Morganna. Instead, he was met with smiles, everyone in town believes that a tornado is the reason behind their town's destruction and death. Which isn't necessarily too far from the truth. The only thing missing is the horde of monsters roaming the streets killing anyone unlucky enough to cross their path. Alex helped as much as he could with people rebuilding their homes and businesses. Survivor's guilt can make a man do crazy things. Thankfully in Alex's case, it made him do compassionate acts of kindness. Which he thinks everyone needs in this moment of devastation.

He would have helped more with the rebuilding process, he wanted too so badly. But fate is a fickle thing and despite his efforts, his parents agreed that it would be safer if they left Shrowl behind. Unlike the rest of the town, they did not forget what happened. They still remembered how Alex fought and won against an unrelenting evil. How Flora was possessed by a three-hundred-year-old witch. But most of all they remembered how they almost lost both of their children when all they wanted was for them to start fresh. With the fortune Alex procured from Eleanor, Donald was able to buy a house down in Saint Augustine, Florida. Not only that but one of the crew members who had quit Witches Treasure managed to get him a job on a sitcom down there. Alex couldn't help but remember how much he wanted to return to Florida. A certain thought came to him, a thought he had first night in Shrowl. He imagined that the next time he saw the glorious white sandy beaches of Florida he'd cry his eyes out, because of how much he'd miss that view. That glorious, peaceful, all-encompassing view. Now when he thinks of that view, he can't help but tear up at the thought of leaving Shrowl. Leaving Liv, and Terry, after everything they have been through. And it (according to Alex) was all for nothing. All that death and destruction despite all odds was for nothing. That thought above all others infuriated him most of all.

***

Alex had just finished packing his bedroom, luckily, he still had most of his things in their boxes when he first moved in. Liv and Terry couldn't help but help out with the move as well. As much as it killed them to do it, they wanted to spend as much time with Alex as they could. Alex stood in his now empty room thinking back to that day he came home beaten and bloody, the day he found the book. He smirked at the closet where the secret cubby was. He did not want to say goodbye to this room but knew he had to. Alex turned at the sound of a knock on the door. It was his mother, she stood awkwardly trying not to make Alex feel worse than he did.

"You okay bud?" she asked. Alex did not answer, words could not describe the level of dread he was feeling right now. "Oh honey, I'm sorry" She embraced her son as he sobbed into her arms. It would have gone on for longer, but it was cut short by the sound of a car horn. "Come on hun, it's time to go" Alex walked closer to the door, his body felt heavier with every step he took. When he finally got to the door, he took one last look into his room and whispered.

"Goodbye Eleanor"

***

As they both walked through the now empty house all the memories they had of this place flooded Alex's mind. Though, sadly most of them he'd rather forget, he'd like to think of all the good that could have happened if they stayed. A brief thought came to him, the thought of the kinds of family events that could have happened in this house. Alex whimpered just at the thought of Flora growing up in a house like this. He didn't care about what had gone on in here, what kind of horrible things happened in this large empty room. All he could see in this moment were missed possibilities, missed futures that would never ever happen. Alex could not help but feel mostly responsible for them leaving. *I should never have found that book, but then again if we hadn't Eleanor's spirit wouldn't be at peace.* So many conflicting thoughts and feelings went through Alex that it was almost unbearable until he heard someone coming into the living room.

It was Terry he looked a lot better than that night when he saved him from Morganna. He was wearing a striped sweater and torn Hot Topic jeans. He too walked in awkwardly not knowing what the right thing to do or say was.

"Can I talk to Alex for a sec Mrs. Host?" he asked gingerly.

She said yes and went outside with the rest. Alex and Terry were now alone in what was once the living room area of the house.

"Is it done?" Alex asked.

"Yes, it's done, the book is buried and it not going anywhere anytime soon."

"Good, and you promise to check on it at least once a week to make sure nobody else finds it, because even though she's gone we can't be certain that there is still some Magik left in that book."

"I know, I know, and I agree with you on all that, okay? But who in their right mind would go looking for something like that?" Terry responded.

"I don't know but it's best that nobody has it, it's too dangerous even if Morganna is gone."

"Agreed" There was a silence between them that was so thick that you could cut it with a knife. Alex just now noticed that Terry had something in his hand, it was a small bracelet.

"I'd take it you're not just in here telling me about what you did with the book?" he asked while pointing at his hand. Terry chuckled and handed him the bracelet.

"I know it's stupid and childish, but I couldn't think of anything else to give you, you don't have to wear it I just wanted you to have it." Terry obliged. Without question, Alex put the bracelet on and tightened it.

"Thank you"

"No, thank you, Alex," Terry interrupted. Before he could get another word in Alex had to interject.

"You shouldn't thank me, because of me you could have—"

"Alex, in case you forgot you saved me and for that, I am forever in your debt so just shut up and be proud of yourself for once. Can you do that? Because if you can't I am not afraid to fly my ass to Florida just so you can see that you are a badass!!!"

"Okay okay I get it."

"No, I don't think you do say it with me, 'I am a badass'."

"Terry I—"

"Shut up and say it" Terry demanded jokingly.

"I'm a badass..." Alex spoke softly.

"LOUDER!!!" Terry shouted. Alex laughed and did what he was told.

"I'M A BADASS!!!" They both laughed hysterically and hugged each other tightly.

"I'm going to miss you dude, give 'em hell down there," Terry said while embracing his friend. Alex chuckled and said bluntly.

"I'm pretty sure I raised enough hell here to last me a lifetime" They both laughed once again. With that interaction, the walk to the front door was much easier than Alex's Walk out of his room.

***

When Alex walked out onto the porch he was met by a familiar face. It was Colin among his family and those involved, he was one of the only people in town who retained his memories of what happened.

"Howdy champ!" he exclaimed. Alex couldn't help but rush into Colin's arms. He had not seen him once in the week that had passed, even in the few days he was in school. Like much of the rest of the town, he had thought he had died too.

"How'd you—" Alex asked. Before he could finish talking Colin answered his question.

"Like you kiddo, I'm a lot tougher than I look" he chuckled as he rustled his hair.

"Colin, what are you doing here?" Alex asked. He smiled, got down on one knee, and spoke.

"I came to see the man you saved my town just before he left" Alex couldn't help but tear up. But there was something that he just now realized. Alex remembered how when he was telling Colin about the vision Eleanor had shown him, he accurately described the small box that contained the stone to which Eleanor's spirit was attached to. As well as the holy silver blade.

"Colin I gotta ask you something and I—" Before he could finish his sentence Colin gazed upon the house, as if he was seeing it for the last time or the first time Alex couldn't tell which.

"Oh, Ellie I knew, deep down I knew you were good," he said to himself.

"You knew?" Alex asked. Colin smiled and continued to gaze upon the house.

"I suppose now is a good time to tell you—"

"Tell me what? Alex asked. Colin smiled and looked at him dead in the eyes. Alex felt somewhat uneasy by this, but he let it play out because he was curious.

"Alex, my real name is Colin Shrowl, my family stayed on this land for generations, I only took my wife's name because I didn't want everyone to assume the worst from me" Alex could not believe what he was hearing Colin is a direct descendent of Eleanor Shrowl. Not once in her visions or her memories does it mention that she had a child. "I guess ole Ellie never mentioned my great-great-great grandfather, did she?" Colin asked jokingly. Alex nodded his head no.

"Oh, well that's okay I only wish I could have been there to see her ya know," Colin said looking at the house in wonder. With that said a thought came to Alex that in his heart knew had to be done. On the front lawn, the moving truck was still there waiting for the okay for them to leave. Alex climbed into the back of the truck and rummaged around to find the one thing out of the whole nightmare he had faced with Morganna he kept. After a minute or two he found it tucked away in the very back of the truck. He then took it out and handed it to Colin. It was the sword, the holy silver blade of Paster Flease that was taken by Eleanor Shrowl which was then used to destroy Morganna Starr. Alex was going to hang it on his wall as some trophy but at this moment he felt that if anyone should have it, it should be the direct descendent of Eleanor herself.

"This sword belonged to Eleanor Shrowl, she gave it to me, and I think you should have it" Alex stated as he handed the sword to Colin. In Colin's hand, he felt as though he was holding a glass, he was that careful when handling this relic. Colin took a deep breath as he gazed into the shining silver hilt of the sword. Alex felt as though he was looking at King Arthur just when he pulled the sword out of the stone. Alex jokingly asked Colin to hold it up like He-Man. Colin couldn't help but oblige. Colin struck a pose and Alex took a picture of him with his phone.

"Alex—I can't I mean you were the one you destroyed Morganna this is yours."

"And now it's yours, Colin" Alex objected, they both smiled, and Colin gave Alex a great big bear hug. "It's the least I can do after you saved my life the day I came here."

"Anytime kiddo, and if you happen to find your way back here give me a call." Alex smiled and nodded. As he was about to close the moving truck, he was tapped on the shoulder, he whipped around and saw Liv.

***

As much as it was a treat to see Liz, in this instance, this was what Alex had been dreading the most. The last time he'll see her. As he looked into her face he studied it once more, so that he would never forget that gorgeous smile, those rosy cheeks, and her piercing blue eyes. The eyes that remind him of the ocean. The ocean that he will never be able to take her on.

"So, here we are..." She smiled. Alex couldn't find the words. Nothing seemed to be good enough, after everything they had been through the word goodbye just was underwhelming for Liv. Not only that but Alex hates goodbyes he didn't always, but right now he did more than ever.

"I uh—" Liv shushed him and kissed Alex deeply on the lips. Every part of Alex felt as though he was in the clouds, it was as if both he and Liv were weightless and there was nothing in the world that could keep them apart. He had proven that just last week when he saved everyone. Alex did not want this moment to end, and when it eventually did it felt like ten-ton bricks fell right back on his shoulders. He caressed her face and she nodded into his arm and kissed his hand.

"Oh shit! I almost forgot!" Alex jumped right back into the moving truck and rummaged through some of his art supplies. He then found something that he had been working on since before Morganna. He picked it up and carefully brought it out of the truck. "Here this is for you," Alex handed Liv the self-portrait he had made of her when they first met. Between the time Alex spent packing, he had used that extra time in-between to finish Liv's drawing. When she held it, she gasped, and her eyes started to get puffy.

"You finished it?" she asked, wiping a tear from her cheek.

"I finished it." Liv grabbed Alex once more and kissed him again.

"I love it, thank you," Liv said while holding Alex in her arms. Alex's chest felt warm, he could feel how fast his heart was beating at that moment. Just like the last moment it eventually ended, only this time it ended when Alex saw his dad with a large bag. It was time to go...

***

Alex and Liv hopped out of the moving truck and gave each other one final hug goodbye. Alex grabbed the bag his dad was carrying and took it to their car.

"Alex, what are you doing with that bag?" Donald asked.

"Taking it to the car, I assume this is my shit, right?"
There was a small silence among them, Donald smiled and
looked at Liv. Something was up, and Alex did not know what
it was.

"Should I tell him, or should you?" Donald asked Liv.

"No, you tell him," Liv responded. Alex's eyes began to
bulge, and his chest was beginning to flutter once more.

"That bag is not for you son, it's for your girlfriend, a
little birdy told me that she had never seen the beach before,
so I thought what harm it would be if I took her on a little
vacation while it was still nice and cool by the beaches. Unless
of course, you don't want her to come along?" Donald asked
jokingly. Alex's heart burst with excitement as he dropped the
bag full of clothes on the ground and rushed over to hug his
dad. He thanked him relentlessly. He then rushed over to Liv
and picked her up and hugged her tighter than he had ever
hugged anyone before. She laughed at Alex's excitement,
which in her eyes looked like a dog going through the
zoomies.

"You knew this was happening?" Alex asked. Liv nodded
through her giggling. "Why did you tell me?"

"So that I could get this reaction" she giggled once
more. Alex felt somewhat stupid right now for being worried
about leaving and he never stopped to think about the
possibility of Liv coming along with them. Granted it was not
permanent, but Alex did not care he got the more time he
wanted with Liv, for him that was the best treasure he could
have. Alex and Liv gave Terry and Colin one last hug goodbye
as they closed the moving truck and did their final checks on
their luggage. Liv and Alex both sat in the very back of the
mini-van and could not keep their hands to themselves. As the
Host family made their way out of the driveway Alex and Liv
waved goodbye out the back window. Though for Alex it
wasn't just a goodbye to his friends it was also a goodbye to
Shrowl entirely.

The Host family moved slowly through the small town of Shrowl Missouri one last time and as they left, they could see that the town was slowly piecing itself back together. Everyone was helping one another, and for Alex, that was the real treasure that he and many others before him had been searching for. The real treasure wasn't gold or silver, it was kindness compassion, and most of all love. Unadulterated, unfiltered, unrelenting love. Alex looked at his family and smiled with pride and then back at Liv who was laying on his chest. Alex Host kissed her on the forehead and felt as though he had found something more priceless than anything in the world. Much like a pirate sailing away with their treasure Alex felt that same feeling when he and his family crossed the town line.

Epilogue

As the Host family made their way out of the county line something else was making its escape as well. Deep within the forests of Shrowl where a once great magnificent cave stood. Lies something much darker than a three-hundred-year-old witch. In the ruins of the cave emerged a dark shadowy cloud that traversed the fallen stone and rubble like a great snake. And much like a snake it was hungry; its hunger was unrelenting. Never satisfied, never resting, and never-ending.

When the black cloud made its way out of the cave fully it burst into the clouds searching for a new home. It scoped the surrounding area like a hawk looking for its next meal. Until finally, it made its choice of where to hide until its next victims arrived. It had found an old, abandoned prison which to its knowledge held one of its many followers. The prison was old and overgrown, one of the walls had been torn down completely much like the cave this was left in ruins. It searched through this maze of halls and empty cells until finally, it came to the lowest point of the prison were stood two corpses both of which looked to have been dead for quite some time. On the ground between them was a Ouija board.

The black cloud felt a presence in this room though this was not the presence of something living it whipped around and saw several people in the room wearing black and white striped suits. One man who stood in the middle of the pack stepped forward. He was tall and lengthy and had a thin complexion.

"What are you?"

"Your salvation" the black cloud hissed.